William M. Thayer

The Bobbin Boy

Outlook

William M. Thayer

The Bobbin Boy

1. Auflage | ISBN: 978-3-73262-860-5

Erscheinungsort: Frankfurt am Main, Deutschland

Erscheinungsjahr: 2018

Outlook Verlag GmbH, Frankfurt.

THE

BOBBIN BOY;

OR,

HOW NAT GOT HIS LEARNING.

AN EXAMPLE FOR YOUTH.

BY

WILLIAM M. THAYER,

AUTHOR OF "THE POOR BOY AND MERCHANT PRINCE," "THE POOR GIRL
AND TRUE WOMAN," "FROM POOR-HOUSE TO PULPIT,"
"TALES FROM THE BIBLE," ETC., ETC.

BOSTON:
J. E. TILTON AND COMPANY.
1862.

University Press, Cambridge:
Printed by Welch, Bigelow, and Company.

PREFACE.

The design of this volume is to show the young how "odd moments" and small opportunities may be used in the acquisition of knowledge. The hero of the tale—N$_{AT}$—is a living character, whose actual boyhood and youth are here delineated—an unusual example of energy, industry, perseverance, application, and enthusiasm in prosecuting a life purpose.

The conclusion of the story will convince the reader, that the group of characters which surround Nat are not creations of the fancy, and that each is the bearer of one or more important lessons to the young. While some of them forcibly illustrate the consequences of idleness, disobedience, tippling, and kindred vices, in youth, others are bright examples of the manly virtues, that always command respect, and achieve success.

W. M. T.

CHAPTER I.

A GOOD BEGINNING.

A little patch of ground enclosed by a fence, a few adjacent trees, Nat with his hoe in hand, his father giving directions, on one of the brightest May mornings that was ever greeted by the carol of birds, are the scenes that open to our view.

"There, Nat, if you plant and hoe your squashes with care, you will raise a nice parcel of them on this piece of ground. It is good soil for squashes."

"How many seeds shall I put into a hill?" inquired Nat.

"Seven or eight. It is well to put in enough, as some of them may not come up, and when they get to growing well, pull up all but four in a hill. You must not have your hills too near together,—they should be five feet apart, and then the vines will cover the ground all over. I should think there would be room for fifty hills on this patch of ground."

"How many squashes do you think I shall raise, father?"

"Well," said his father, smiling, "that is hard telling. We won't count the chickens before they are hatched. But if you are industrious, and take very good care indeed of your vines, stir the ground often and keep out all the weeds, and kill the bugs, I have little doubt that you will get well paid for your labor."

"If I have fifty hills," said Nat, "and four vines in each hill, I shall have two hundred vines in all; and if there is one squash on each vine, there will be two hundred squashes."

"Yes; but there are so many *ifs* about it that you may be disappointed after all. Perhaps the bugs will destroy half your vines."

"I can kill the bugs," said Nat.

"Perhaps dry weather will wither them all up."

"I can water them every day if they need it."

"That is certainly having good courage, Nat," added his father, "but if you conquer the bugs, and get around the dry weather, it may be too wet and blast your vines, or there may be such a hail storm as I have known several times in my life, and cut them to pieces."

"I don't think there will be such a hail storm this year; there never was one like it since I can remember.”

“I hope there won’t be,” replied his father. “It is well to look on the bright side, and hope for the best for it keeps the courage up. It is also well to look out for disappointment. I know a gentleman who thought he would raise some ducks. So he obtained a dozen eggs, and put them under a hen, and then he hired a man, to make a small artificial pond in his garden, which he could fill from his well, for the young ducks to swim in. The time came for the ducks to appear, but not one of the eggs hatched, and it caused much merriment among the neighbors, and the man has never heard the last of *counting ducks before they are hatched*. I have heard people in the streets and stores say, when some one was undertaking a doubtful enterprise, ‘he is counting ducks.’ Now, possibly, your squashes may turn out like the gentleman’s ducks, though I do not really think it will be so. I speak of it that you may think of these things.”

A sly sort of smile played over Nat’s expressive countenance at this mention of the ducks, but it did not shake his confidence in the art of raising squashes. He had become a thorough believer in squashes,—they were now a part of his creed. He could see them on the vines before the seeds were planted. Some of them were very large,—as big as a water-pail, and his glowing imagination set him to work already, rolling them into a wheelbarrow. He cared little for the bugs, though they should come in a great army, he could conquer them, infantry, artillery, and all.

This scene was enacted about thirty-five years ago, not a thousand miles from Boston, when Nat was about ten years old, a bright, active, energetic, efficient, hopeful little fellow. His father gave him the use of a piece of ground for raising squashes, and the boy was to have the proceeds of the crop with which to line his new purse. Nat was wont to look on the bright side of things, and it was generally fair weather with him. For this reason, he expected a good crop of squashes, notwithstanding his father’s adverse hints. It was fortunate for him that he was so hopeful, for it inspired him with zeal and earnestness, and made him more successful than he otherwise would have been. All hopeful persons are not successful, but nearly all the successful ones, in the various callings of life, were hopeful from the beginning. This was true of Nathaniel Bowditch, the great mathematician, who was a poor boy when he commenced his studies. He said that whenever he undertook any thing “it never occurred to him for a moment that he could fail.” This quality thus encouraged him to press on from one success to another. Hence, in later life, his counsel to youth was, “Never undertake any thing but with the feeling that you can and will do it. With that feeling success is certain, and without it failure is unavoidable.” He once said that it had been an invariable rule with him, “to do one thing at a time, and to *finish* whatever he began.” The same was true of Sir Humphrey Davy. His biographer says that he never made any provision for failures, "that he undertook every experiment as if success were certain." This put life and soul into his acts; for when a man believes that he shall certainly succeed in a given work, his success is half secured. Grave doubts about it diminish energy, and relax the force of the will. Buxton, the distinguished English philanthropist, is another example of this quality. He was just as confident that his efforts in behalf of the oppressed would succeed, as he was of his own existence. He knew that God and truth were on his side, and therefore he expected to triumph,—and he did. We shall see that Nat was often helped by his hopefulness.

It was a happy day to Nat when he saw his squashes coming forth to seek the genial light. Frank Martin was with him when the discovery was made, and it brightened Nat's hope considerably, if it be possible to make a bright thing brighter.

"Here, Frank, they are coming. There is one—two—three—"

"Sure enough," answered Frank, "they will all show themselves soon. You will raise a lot of squashes on this patch of ground. You will have to drive a team to Boston market to carry them, likely as not."

"I hardly think father expects to see any squashes of *my* raising," said Nat.

"Why not?" inquired Frank.

"Oh, he is expecting the bugs will eat them up, or that it will be too wet or too dry, or that a hail storm will cut them to pieces, or something else will destroy them; I hardly know what."

"You will fare as well as other folks, I guess," added Frank. "If anybody has squashes this year, you will have them; I am certain of that. But it will take most of your time out of school to hoe them, and keep the weeds out."

"I don't care for that, though I think I can take care of them mornings by getting up early, and then I can play after school."

"Then you mean to play some yet?"

"Of course I do. I shouldn't be a boy if I didn't play, though father says I shouldn't believe in all play and no work."

"You don't. If you work in the morning and play at night, that is believing in both, and I think it is about fair."

"Ben Drake was along here when I was planting my squashes," said Nat, "and he told me that I was a fool to worry myself over a lot of squash vines, and have no time to play. He said he wouldn't do it for a cart-load of squashes."

"And what did you tell him?" asked Frank.

"I told him that father thought it was better for boys to work some, and form the habit of being industrious, and learn how to do things; for then they would be more successful when they became men."

"What did Ben say to that?"

"'Just like an old man!' he said. 'It is time enough to work when we get to be men. I should like to see myself taking care of a garden when the other boys are playing.' By this time," continued Nat, "I thought I would put in a word, so I told him that it would be good for *him* to work part of the time, and I had heard a number of people say so. He was quite angry at this, and said, 'it was nobody's business, he should work when he pleased.' 'So shall I,' I replied, 'and I please to work on these squashes part of my time, whether Ben Drake thinks well of it or not.'"

We shall see hereafter what kind of a boy this Ben was (everybody called him Ben instead of Benjamin), and what kind of a man he made.

Nat expressed his opinion rather bluntly, although he was not a forward, unmannerly boy. But he usually had an opinion of his own, and was rather distinguished for "thinking (as a person said of him since) on his own hook." When he was only four years old, and was learning to read little words of two letters, he came across one about which he had quite a dispute with his teacher. It was INN.

"What is that?" asked his teacher.

"I-double n," he answered.

"What does i-double n spell?"

"Tavern," was his quick reply.

The teacher smiled, and said, "No; it spells INN. Now read it again."

"I-double n—tavern," said he.

"I told you that it did not spell tavern, it spells INN. Now pronounce it correctly."

"It *do* spell tavern," said he.

The teacher was finally obliged to give it up, and let him enjoy his own opinion. She probably called him obstinate, although there was nothing of the kind about him, as we shall see. His mother took up the matter at home, but failed to convince him that i-double n did not spell tavern. It was not until some time after, that he changed his opinion on this important subject.

That this incident was no evidence of obstinacy in Nat, but only of a disposition to think "on his own hook," is evident from the following circumstances. There was a picture of a public-house in his book against the word INN, with the old-fashioned sign-post in front, on which a sign was swinging. Near his father's, also, stood a public-house, which everybody called a *tavern*, with a tall post and sign in front of it, exactly like that in his book; and Nat said within himself, if Mr. Morse's house (the landlord) is a tavern, then this is a tavern in my book. He cared little how it was spelled; if it did not spell tavern, "*it ought to*," he thought. Children believe what they *see*, more than what they hear. What they lack in reason and judgment, they make up in eyes. So Nat had seen the *tavern* near his father's house, again and again, and he had stopped to look at the sign in front of it a great many times, and his eyes told him it was just like that in the book; therefore it was his deliberate opinion that i-double n spelt tavern, and he was not to be beaten out of an opinion that was based on such clear evidence. It was a good sign in Nat. It is a characteristic of nearly every person who lives to make a mark upon the world. It was true of the three men, to whom we have just referred, Bowditch, Davy, and Buxton. From their childhood they thought for themselves, so that when they became men, they defended their opinions against imposing opposition. True, a youth must not be too forward in advancing his ideas, especially if they do not harmonize with those of older persons. Self-esteem and self-confidence should be guarded against. Still, in avoiding these evils, he is not obliged to believe any thing just because he is told so. It is better for him to understand the reason of things, and believe them on that account.

But to return to Ben Drake. To Nat's last remark he replied, endeavoring to ridicule him for undertaking an enterprise on so small a scale,

"If I was going to work at all, I wouldn't putter over a few hills of squashes, I can tell you. It is too small business. I'd do something or nothing."

"What great thing *would* you do? asked Nat.

"I would go into a store, and sell goods to ladies and gentlemen, and wear nice clothes."

"And be nothing but a waiter to everybody for awhile. Fred Jarvis is only an errand-boy in Boston."

"I know that, but *I* wouldn't be a waiter for anybody, and do the sweeping, making fires and carrying bundles; I don't believe in 'nigger's' work, though I think that is better than raising squashes."

"I don't think it is small business at all to do what Fred Jarvis is doing, or to raise squashes," replied Nat. "I didn't speak of Fred because I thought he was doing something beneath him. I think that 'niggers' work is better than laziness;" and the last sentence was uttered in a way that seemed rather personal to Ben.

"Well," said Ben, as he cut short the conversation and hurried away, "if you wish to be a bug-killer this summer, you may for all me, I shan't."

Ben belonged to a class of boys who think it is beneath their dignity to do some necessary and useful work. To carry bundles, work in a factory, be nothing but a farmer's boy, or draw a hand-cart, is a compromise of dignity, they think. Nat belonged to another class, who despise all such ridiculous notions. He was willing to do any thing that was necessary, though some people might think it was degrading. He did not feel above useful employment, on the farm, or in the workshop and factory. And this quality was a great help to him. For it is cousin to that hopefulness which he possessed, and brother to his self-reliance and independence. No man ever accomplished much who was afraid of doing work beneath his dignity. Dr. Franklin was nothing but a soap-boiler when he commenced; Roger Sherman was only a cobbler, and kept a book by his side on the bench; Ben Jonson was a mason and worked at his trade, with a trowel in one hand and a book in the other; John Hunter, the celebrated physiologist, was once a carpenter, working at day labor; John Foster was a weaver in his early life, and so was Dr. Livingstone, the missionary traveller; an American President was a hewer of wood in his youth, and hence he replied to a person who asked him what was his coat of arms, "A pair of shirt sleeves;" Washington was a farmer's boy, not ashamed to dirty his hands in cultivating the soil; John Opie, the renowned English portrait painter, sawed wood for a living before he became professor of painting in the Royal Academy; and hundreds of other distinguished men commenced their career in business no more respectable; but not one of them felt that dignity was compromised by their humble vocation. They believed that honor crowned all the various branches of industry, however discreditable they might appear to some, and that disgrace would eventually attach to any one who did not act well his part in the most popular pursuit. Like them, Nat was never troubled with mortification on account of his poverty, or the humble work he was called upon to do. His sympathies were rather inclined in the other direction, and, other things being equal, the sons of the poor and humble were full as likely to share his attentions.

We are obliged to pass over much that belongs to the patch of squashes—the many hours of hard toil that it cost Nat to bring the plants to maturity,—the two-weeks' battle with the bugs when he showed himself a thorough Napoleon to conquer the enemy,—the spicy compliments he received for his industry and success in gardening,—the patient waiting for the rain-drops to fall in dry weather, and for the sun to shine forth in his glory when it was too wet,—the intimate acquaintance he cultivated with every squash, knowing just their number and size,—and many other things that show the boy.

The harvest day arrived,—the squashes were ripe,—and a fine parcel of them there was. Nat was satisfied with the fruit of his labor, as he gathered them for the market.

"What a pile of them!" exclaimed Frank, as he came over to see the squashes after school. "You are a capital gardener, Nat; I don't believe there is a finer lot of squashes in town."

"Father says the bugs and dry weather couldn't hold out against my perseverance," added Nat, laughing. "But the next thing is to sell them."

"Are you going to carry them to Boston?" asked Frank.

"No; I shall sell them in the village. Next Saturday afternoon I shall try my luck."

"You will turn peddler then?"

"Yes; but I don't think I shall like it so well as raising the squashes. There is real satisfaction in seeing them grow."

"If you can peddle as well as you can garden it, you will make a real good hand at it; and such handsome squashes as those ought to go off like hot cakes."

Saturday afternoon came, and Nat started with his little cart full of squashes. He was obliged to be his own horse, driver, and salesman, in which threefold capacity he served with considerable ability.

"Can I sell you some squashes to-day?" said Nat to the first neighbor on whom he called.

"Squashes! where did you find such fine squashes as those?" asked the neighbor, coming up to the cart, and viewing the contents.

"I raised them," said Nat; "and I have a good many more at home."

"What! did you plant and hoe them, and take the whole care of them?"

"Yes, sir; no one else struck a hoe into them, and I am to have all the money they bring."

"You deserve it, Nat, every cent of it. I declare, you beat me completely; for the bugs eat mine all up, so that I did not raise a decent squash. How did you keep the bugs off?"

"I killed thousands of them," said Nat. "In the morning before I went to school I looked over the vines; when I came home at noon I spent a few moments in killing them, and again at night I did the same. They troubled me only about two weeks."

"Well, they troubled *me* only two weeks," replied the neighbor, "and by that time there was nothing left for them to trouble. But very few boys like to work well enough to do what you have done, and very few have the patience to do it either. With most of the boys it is all play and no work. But what do you ask for your squashes?"

Nat proceeded to answer: "That one is worth six cents; such a one as that eight; that is ten; and a big one like that (holding up the largest) is fifteen."

The neighbor expressed his approval of the prices, and bought a number of them, for which he paid him the money. Nat went on with his peddling tour, calling at every house in his way; and he met with very good success. Just as he turned the corner of a street on the north side of the common, Ben Drake discovered him, and shouted, "Hurrah for the squash-peddler! That is tall business, Nat; don't you feel grand? What will you take for your horse?"

Nat made no reply, but hastened on to the next house where he disposed of all the squashes that he carried but two. He soon sold them, and returned home to tell the story of his first peddling trip. Once or twice afterwards he went on the same errand, and succeeded very well. But he became weary of the business, for some reason, before he sold all the squashes, and he hit upon this expedient to finish the work.

"Sis," said he to a sister younger than himself, "I will give you one of my pictures for every squash you will sell. You can carry three or four at a time easy enough."

Sis accepted the proposition with a good deal of pleasure; for she was fond of drawings, and Nat had some very pretty ones. He possessed a natural taste for drawing, and he had quite a collection of birds, beasts, houses, trees, and other objects, drawn and laid away carefully in a box. For a boy of his age, he was really quite an artist. His squashes were not better than his drawings. His patience, perseverance, industry, and self-reliance, made him successful both as a gardener and artist.

In a few days, "Sis" had sold the last squash, and received her pay, according to the agreement. The sequel will show that peddling squashes was the only enterprise which Nat undertook and failed to carry through. His failure there is quite unaccountable, when you connect it with every other part of his life.

We are reminded that many men of mark commenced their career by peddling. The great English merchant, Samuel Budgett, when he was about ten years old, went out into the streets to sell a bird, in order that he might get some funds to aid his poor mother. The first money that Dr. Kitto obtained was the proceeds of the sale of *labels*, which he made and peddled from shop to shop. One of the wealthiest men we know, a Christian man distinguished for his large benevolence, commenced his mercantile career by peddling goods that he carried in a band-box from one milliner's shop to another. "You must creep before you can walk," is an old maxim, and the lives of all distinguished men verify the proverb. He who creeps well, will walk so much the better by and by; but he who is ashamed to creep, must never expect to walk. We know a successful merchant who commenced the work of an errand-boy in a large mercantile house, when he was about twelve years old. He was not mortified to be caught with a bundle in hand in the street, nor to be seen sweeping the store. Not feeling above his business, he discharged his duties as well as he could. When he swept he swept,—every nook and corner was thoroughly cleaned out. When he carried a bundle, he carried it,—nimbly, manfully, promptly, and politely he went and delivered it. He performed these little things so well that he was soon promoted to a more important post. Here, too, he was equally faithful and thorough, and his employers saw that he possessed just the qualities to insure success. They promoted him again; and before he was twenty years old he was the head clerk of the establishment. He was not much past his majority when he was admitted as a partner to the firm; and now he stands at the head of the well-known house, a man of affluence, intelligence, and distinction. Had he been ashamed to carry a bundle or sweep a store when he was a boy, by this time his friends would have had abundant reason to be ashamed of him.

This chapter of Nat's early experience in squash culture, was quite unimportant at the time. It is still only a memorial of *boyish* days; but it was a good beginning. It shows as clearly as the most distinguished service he afterwards rendered to his fellow men, that hopefulness, industry, perseverance, economy of time, self-reliance, and other valuable traits, were elements of his character.

CHAPTER II.

UPWARD AND ONWARD.

It was winter,—about three months after the sale of the squashes. The district school was in progress, and a male teacher presided over it.

"Scholars," said the teacher one day, "it is both pleasant and profitable to have an occasional declamation and dialogue spoken in school. It will add interest, also, to our spelling-school exercises in the evening. Now who would like to participate in these exercises?"

Nat was on his feet in a moment; for he was always ready to declaim, or perform his part of a dialogue. The teacher smiled to see such a little fellow respond so readily, and he said to Nat,

"Did you ever speak a piece?"

"Yes, sir, a good many times."

"Do you like to declaim?"

"Yes, sir, and speak dialogues too."

"What piece did you ever speak?"

"'My voice is still for war,'" replied Nat.

"A great many boys have spoken that," added the teacher, amused at Nat's hearty approval of the plan.

"Will you select a piece to-night, and show it to me to-morrow morning?" he asked.

"Yes, sir; and learn it too," answered Nat.

Only four or five scholars responded to the teacher's proposition, and Frank Martin was one, Nat's "right hand man" in all studies and games. The teacher arranged with each one for a piece, and the school was dismissed. As soon as school was out.

"Frank," said Nat, "will you speak 'ALEXANDER THE GREAT AND A ROBBER' with me?"

"Yes, if the teacher is willing. Which part will you take?"

"The 'robber,' if you are willing to be great Alexander."

Frank agreed to the proposition, and as the dialogue was in Pierpont's First

Class Book, which was used in school, they turned to it, and showed it to the teacher before he left the school-house. It was arranged that they should speak it on the next day, provided they could commit it in so short a time.

"Going to speak a dialogue to-morrow," said Nat to his mother, as he went into the house.

"What are you going to speak?"

"Alexander the Great and a Robber," replied Nat. "And I shall be the robber, and Frank will be Alexander."

"Why do you choose to be the robber?" inquired his mother. "I hope you have no inclination that way."

"I like that part," replied Nat, "because the robber shows that the king is as much of a robber as himself. The king looks down upon him with scorn, and calls him a robber; and then the robber tells the king that he has made war upon people, and robbed them of their property, homes, and wives and children, so that he is a worse robber than himself. The king hardly knows what to say, and the last thing the robber says to him is, 'I believe neither you nor I shall ever atone to the world for half the mischief we have done it.' Then the king orders his chains to be taken off, and says, 'Are we then so much alike? Alexander like a robber?'"

"That is a very good reason, I think, for liking that part," said his mother. "Many people do not stop to think that the great can be guilty of crimes. They honor a king or president whether he has any principle or not."

"That is what I like to see exposed in the dialogue," said Nat. "It is just as bad for a king to rob a person of all he has, in war, as it is for a robber to do it at midnight."

Nat always felt strongly upon this point. He very early learned that rich men, and those occupying posts of honor, were thought more of by many people, whether they were deserving or not, and it seemed to him wrong. He thought that one good boy ought to stand just as high as another, though his parents were poor and humble, and that every man should bear the guilt of his own deeds whether he be king or servant. Out of this feeling grew his interest in the aforesaid dialogue, and he was willing to take the place of the robber for the sake of the pleasure of "showing up" the king. It was this kind of feeling that caused him to sympathize, even when a boy, with objects of distress and suffering,—to look with pity upon those who experienced misfortune, or suffered reproach unjustly. It was not strange that he became a professed Democrat in his youth, as we shall see; for how could such a democratic little fellow be other than a true Jeffersonian Democrat?

Nat's part of the dialogue was committed on that evening before eight o'clock. He could commit a piece very quick, for he learned any thing easily. He could repeat many of the lessons of his reading book, word for word. His class had read them over a number of times, so that he could repeat them readily. At the appointed time, on the next afternoon, both Nat and Frank were ready to perform.

"I have the pleasure this afternoon," said the teacher, "to announce a dialogue by two of the boys who volunteered yesterday. Now if they shall say it without being prompted, you will all concede that they have done nobly to commit it so quickly Let us have it perfectly still. The title of the dialogue is 'Alexander the Great and a Robber.' Now boys, we are ready."

Frank commenced in a loud, pompous, defiant tone, that was really Alexander-like. It was evident from the time he uttered the first sentence that, if he could not be "Alexander the Great," he could be Alexander the Little.

Nat responded, and performed his part with an earnestness of soul, a power of imitation, and a degree of eloquence that surprised the teacher. The scholars were not so much surprised because they had heard him before, but it was the first time the teacher had seen him perform.

"Very well done," said the teacher, as they took their seats. "There could not be much improvement upon that. You may repeat the dialogue at the spelling-school on Friday evening; and I hope both of you will have declamations next week."

"*I* will, sir," said Nat.

The teacher found a reluctance among the boys to speak, and one of them said to him,

"If I could speak as well as Nat, I would do it."

This remark caused him to think that Nat's superiority in these rhetorical exercises might dishearten some of his pupils; and the next time he introduced the subject to the school, he took occasion to remark,

"Some of our best orators were very poor speakers when they began to declaim in boyhood. It is not certain that a lad who does not acquit himself very well in this exercise at first, will not make a good orator at last. Demosthenes, who was the most gifted orator of antiquity, had an impediment in his speech in early life. But he determined to overcome it, and be an orator in spite of it. He tried various expedients, and finally went to a cave daily, on the sea-shore, where, with pebble-stones in his mouth, he declaimed, until the impediment was removed. By patience and perseverance he became a renowned orator. It was somewhat so, too, with Daniel Webster, whom you all know as the greatest orator of our land and times. The first time he went upon the stage to speak, he was so frightened that he could not recall the first line of his piece. The second time he did not do much better; and it was not until he had made several attempts, that he was able to get through a piece tolerably well. But a strong determination and persevering endeavors, finally gave him success."

In the course of the winter Nat spoke a number of pieces, among which were "Marco Bozzaris," "Speech of Catiline before the Roman Senate on Hearing his Sentence of Banishment," and "Dialogue from Macbeth," in all of which he gained himself honor. His taste seemed to prefer those pieces in which strength and power unite. At ten and twelve years of age, he selected such declamations and dialogues as boys generally do at the age of sixteen or eighteen years. It was not unusual for the teacher to say, when visitors were in school,

"Come, Master —— [Nat], can you give us a declamation?" and Nat was never known to refuse. He always had one at his tongue's end, which would roll off, at his bidding, as easily as thread unwinds from a spool.

About this time there was some complaint among the scholars in Nat's arithmetic class, and Samuel Drake persuaded one of the older boys to write a petition to the teacher for shorter lessons. This Samuel Drake was a brother of Ben, a bad boy, as we shall see hereafter, known in the community as Sam. When the petition was written, Sam signed it, and one or two other boys did the same; but when he presented it to Nat, the latter said,

"What should I sign that for? The lessons are not so long as I should like to have them. Do you study them any in the evening?"

"Study in the evening!" exclaimed Sam. "I am not so big a fool as that. It is bad enough to study in school."

"I study evenings," added Nat, "and you are as able to study as I am. The lessons would be too long for me if I didn't study any."

"And so you don't mean to sign this petition?" inquired Sam.

"Of course I don't," replied Nat. "If the lessons are not too long, there is no reason why I should petition to have them shorter."

"You can sign it for our sakes," pleaded Sam.

"Not if I think you had better study them as they are."

"Go to grass then," said Sam, becoming angry, "we can get along without a squash peddler, I'd have you know. You think you are of mighty consequence, and after you have killed a few more bugs perhaps you will be."

"I won't sign your petition," said Frank, touched to the quick by this abuse of Nat.

"Nor I," exclaimed Charlie Stone, another intimate associate of Nat's, and a good scholar too.

Nat was sensitive to ridicule when it proceeded from certain persons, but he did not care much for it when its author was Sam Drake, a boy whom every teacher found dull and troublesome. He replied, however, in a pleasant though sarcastic manner, addressing his remark to Frank and Charlie,

"Sam is so brilliant that he expects to get along without study. He will be governor yet."

Sam did not relish this thrust very much, but before he had a chance to reply, Frank added, "I suppose you will make a speech, Sam, when you present your petition." All laughed heartily at this point, and turned away, leaving Sam to bite his lips and cogitate.

Sam was certainly in a predicament. He had several signers to his petition, but they were all the lazy, backward scholars, and he knew it. To send a petition to the teacher with these signatures alone, he knew would be little less than an insult. If Nat, Frank, and Charlie, would have signed it, he would not have hesitated. As it was, he did not dare to present it, so the petition movement died because it couldn't live.

The teacher, however, heard of the movement, and some days thereafter, thinking that his dull scholars might need a word of encouragement, he embraced a favorable opportunity to make the following remarks:—

"It is not always the case that the brightest scholars in boyhood make the most useful or learned men. There are many examples of distinguished men, who were very backward scholars in youth. The great philosopher Newton was one of the dullest scholars in school when he was twelve years old. Doctor Isaac Barrow was such a dull, pugnacious, stupid fellow, that his father was heard to say, if it pleased God to remove any one of his children by death, he hoped it would be Isaac. The father of Doctor Adam Clarke, the commentator, called his boy 'a grievous dunce.' Cortina, a renowned painter, was nicknamed, by his associates, 'Ass' Head,' on account of his stupidity, when a boy. When the mother of Sheridan once went with him to the school-room, she told the teacher that he was 'an incorrigible dunce,' and the latter was soon compelled to believe her. One teacher sent Chatterton home to his mother as 'a fool of whom nothing could be made.' Napoleon and Wellington were both backward scholars. And Sir Walter Scott was named the 'The Great Blockhead' at school. But some of these men, at a certain period of youth, changed their course of living, and began to apply themselves with great earnestness and assiduity to the acquisition of knowledge, while others, though naturally dull, improved their opportunities from the beginning, and all became renowned. No one of them advanced without close application. It was by their own persevering efforts that they finally triumphed over all difficulties. So it must be with yourselves. The dullest scholar in this room may distinguish himself by application and dint of perseverance, while the brightest may fail of success, by wasting his time and trusting to his genius. The motto of every youth should be 'UPWARD AND ONWARD.'"

CHAPTER III.

SATURDAY AFTERNOON.

The bright summer-time had come again, when the sweet-scented blossoms beautified the gardens, and the forming fruits gave promise of a rich golden harvest. The school-bell sent out its merry call to the laughing children, and scores of them daily went up to the temple of knowledge for improvement. Saturday afternoon was a season of recreation, when the pupils, released from school, engaged in various sports, or performed some light labor for their parents.

On a certain Saturday afternoon, Nat, Charlie, Frank, and one or two other boys, arranged for a "good time" at the house of one of the number. They were all there promptly at the appointed time, together with Frank's little dog Trip— a genuine favorite with all the boys who had any regard for dog- brightness and amiability.

"Look here, Frank, has Trip forgot how to play hy-spy?" asked Charlie.

"No; he will play it about as well as *you* can. Let us try it."

"You can't learn him to touch the goal, can you?" inquired another boy.

"No," replied Frank; "but I expect he will before he takes his degree. He is nothing but a Freshman now."

"Did he ever petition you for shorter lessons?" asked Nat.

Charlie and Frank laughed; for they thought of Sam Drake's petition at the winter school.

"Never," answered Frank; "but he has asked me for longer ones a great many times. He never gets enough at any sport. He will play 'hide and seek' or 'ball' as long as you will want to have him, and then wag his tail for more."

Trip sat by looking wistfully up into his little master's face as if he perfectly understood the praise that was lavished upon him, and was patiently waiting to give an exhibition of his skill in athletic games.

"Let us try his skill," said Charlie. "Come, Frank, give him his post."

"Here, Trip," said Frank, "come here; nice fellow,—does want to play 'hide and seek;' so he shall;" and he patted him on his head, for which kindness Trip voted him thanks as well as he could.

"Now, boys, we'll all run and hide, and Trip will find us in short metre."

Off they started, some round the barn and house, and some over the wall, while Trip stood wagging his tail, in the spot assigned him. At length a loud shrill "whoop," "whoop," "whoop," one after another, saluted Trip's ears, and off he ran to find them. Bounding over the wall, he came right upon Charlie, who laughed heartily at the result, while Trip extended his researches round the barn, where he discovered Nat under a pile of boards, and one or two of the other boys. When they all returned to the goal, Trip perceived that his master was not found, and off he bounded a second time.

"Sure enough," exclaimed Charlie, "he knows that Frank is not here, and he has gone to find him. Isn't he a knowing dog?"

"I don't believe he will find him," said Nat, "for he is up on a beam in the shed."

Nat had scarcely uttered these words, before a shout from Frank and a bark from Trip announced that the former was discovered.

"There," said Frank, as he came up to the goal with Trip skipping and jumping at his side, "wasn't that well done? I told you he would find you, and none of us could do it quicker."

"Let us try it again," said one of the boys, "I guess I'll puzzle him this time."

Again they all sought hiding-places, while Trip waited at the goal for the well-known signal—"whoop;" "whoop;" "whoop." None of the boys knew the meaning of this better than he, although he was only a dog.

Soon the signal was given, and away went Trip in high glee. Over the wall—around the barn—into the shed—back of the house—behind the woodpile—under the boards—here and there—he ran until every boy was found. Again and again the experiment was tried, and Trip won fresh laurels every time.

"You've torn your pants, Nat," said Frank.

"I know it. I did it getting over the fence. I haven't done such a thing before, I don't know when."

While exhausting "hy-spy" of its fun, Sylvester Jones came along with a bit of news.

"Going to court, Nat?" he inquired.

"Going where?" replied Nat, not understanding him.

"*To court*! They have taken up Harry Gould and Tom Ryder, and the court is coming off at the hall."

"What have they taken Harry and Tom for?" asked Nat, becoming deeply interested in the event.

"I don't know exactly; but it is something about disturbing the exhibition."

The facts in the case were these. There was an exhibition in the hall owned by the manufacturing company, and these two boys climbed up on the piazza and looked into the window, thereby disturbing the exercises. An action was brought against them, and they were to be tried before a justice of the town.

"It is too bad," replied Nat, "to take up such little boys for *that*—they didn't know any better. What will be done with them, do you expect?"

"Perhaps they will send them to jail. Father says it is a serious matter to disturb a meeting of any kind."

"Yes," replied Nat, "it is a mean act in anybody, but I don't believe that Harry and Tom understood it. It will be too bad to send them to prison for that. Perhaps they would never do such a thing again."

"Come," added Sylvester, "let us go to the trial and see. They have begun before this time."

Nat's sympathies were intensely wrought upon by these tidings; for Harry and Tom were among his school-fellows. The idea of trying such little boys in a court of justice excited him very much. He forgot all about the games projected and the rent in his pantaloons, and seizing his cap, he said to Frank,

"Will *you* go?"

"Yes, I've played about enough," answered Frank. "I would like to go to a court."

The boys hurried away to the hall; and they found that the court had opened, and that the room was well filled with people. Nat edged his way along through the crowd until he found himself directly in front of the table where the justice sat. Sure enough, there the two young prisoners were, Harry and Tom, looking as if they were half frightened out of their wits. How Nat pitied them! It seemed strange to him that men could deal thus with boys so small. He listened to the examination, of witnesses with great emotion, and watched Harry and Tom so closely that he could read their very thoughts. He knew just how badly they felt, and that if they could get clear this time, they never would be caught in such wrong-doing again.

"Were you present at the exhibition?" inquired the justice of one of the witnesses.

"I was," he answered.

"Did the prisoners disturb the exercise?"

"They did."

"How do you know that Harry and Tom were the boys?"

"Because I went out to send them away, and found them on the piazza."

"Did you speak to them, and call them by name, so that you could not be mistaken?"

"I did, and they responded to their names."

"Then you can swear that these two boys, the prisoners, disturbed the meeting?"

"Yes, I am positive of it."

Two or three other witnesses were examined, when the justice said,

"It appears to be a clear case, boys, that you are guilty of the charges alleged against you. You are very young to begin to disturb the public peace. Even if it was nothing but thoughtlessness, boys are getting to be so rude, that it is high time some check was put upon their mischief. Now, boys, have you any thing to say for yourselves?"

Harry and Tom were more frightened than ever, and Nat could see them struggle to keep from crying outright.

"Have you any one to speak for you?" asked the justice.

Nat could withstand it no longer, and he stepped forward, with his cap in his hand, his bright eyes beaming with sympathy for the prisoners, and said,

"Please, sir, I will speak for them, if you are willing," and without waiting for the justice to reply, he proceeded:

"Harry and Tom would never do the like again. They knew it was wrong for them to disturb the exhibition, but they didn't think. They *will* think next time. I know they feel sorry now for what they have done, and will try to be good boys hereafter. Can you not try them, if they will promise? This is the first time they have done so, and they will promise, I know they will (turning to the boys), won't you, Tom?"

The boys both nodded assent, and the justice looked pleased, astonished, and not a little puzzled. It was really a scene for the artist, Nat standing before the court with cap in hand, and his pantaloons torn in the play of the afternoon, his heart so moved with pity for the juvenile offenders that he almost forgot where he was, making a touching plea for the boys, as if their destiny depended upon his own exertions. The hall was so still that the fall of a pin might be heard while Nat was pleading the case. Everybody was taken by surprise. They could hardly believe their senses.

"Their brother," answered one man, in reply to the inquiry, "Who is that lad?" He did not know himself, but he thought that possibly a brother might plead thus for them.

The justice was not long in deciding the case, after such a plea. He simply reprimanded the two boys, gave them some wholesome counsel, and discharged them, much to the gratification of Nat, and many others.

"That was the youngest lawyer I ever heard plead a case," said Mr. Payson, after the court adjourned.

"The most impudent one, *I* think," replied Mr. Sayles, to whom the remark was addressed. "If I had been in the place of the justice, I would have kicked him out of the hall. Little upstart! to come in there, and presume to speak in behalf of two reckless boys!"

"You misjudge the boy entirely, Mr. Sayles. There is nothing of the 'upstart' about Nat. He is a good boy, a good scholar, and very amiable indeed. The neighbors will all tell you so. It was his sincere pity for the boys that led him to plead for them. He did not mean to conceal their guilt, but he thought, as *I* do, that such small boys better be reproved and tried again, before they suffer the penalty of the law."

"I hope it is so," replied Mr. S.

"I *know* it is so," continued Mr. P. "Nat is very kind and sympathizing, and he cannot endure to see a dog abused. It might seem bold and unmannerly for him to address the court as he did, but Nat is not such a boy. He is very mannerly for one of his age, and nothing but his deep pity for Harry and Tom induced him to speak. The act has elevated him considerably in my estimation, though I thought well of him before."

Mr. Payson took the right view of the matter. In addition to his sympathy for his school-fellows, Nat felt that it was hardly right to take those little boys before a court for the offence charged, since they were not vagrants, and were not known as bad boys. If Ben and Sam Drake had been there instead of Harry and Tom, he would not have volunteered a plea to save them from the clutches of the law. But he felt that it was dealing too severely with them, and this emboldened him, so that when he witnessed the distress of the boys, and saw them try to conceal their emotions, his heart overflowed with pity for them, and forced him to speak.

If we knew nothing more of Nat, this single act would lead us to anticipate that, in later life, he would espouse the cause of the oppressed in every land, and lift his voice and use his pen in defence of human rights. At the age of ten or twelve years, John Howard, the philanthropist, was not distinguished above the mass of boys around him, except for the kindness of his heart, and boyish deeds of benevolence. It was so with Wilberforce, whose efforts in the cause of British emancipation gave him a world-wide fame. Every form of suffering, misfortune, or injustice, touched his young heart, and called forth some expression of tender interest. Carefully he would lay off his shoes at the door of a sick chamber, and often divide a small coin, received as a present, between his own wants and some poor child or man he chanced to meet. And Buxton, whose self-sacrificing spirit in behalf of suffering humanity is everywhere known, was early observed by his mother to sympathize with the down-trodden and unfortunate, and she sought to nurture and develop this feeling as a hopeful element of character. When his fame was at its zenith, he wrote to his mother, "I constantly feel, especially in action and exertion for others, the effects of principles early implanted by you in my mind."

CHAPTER IV.

THE WILD CHERRIES

Nat, Charlie, and Frank planned a pleasure excursion one Saturday afternoon, when cherries were in their prime. They did not even think of the cherries, however, when they planned the trip. They thought more of the fields and forests through which they proposed to go. But just at this point one of their associates came up, and said,

"Let us go over beyond Capt. Pratt's and get some cherries. There is a large tree there, and it hangs full."

"Yes; and have the owner in your hair," answered Charlie.

"No, no," replied John, the name of the boy who made the proposition. "They are *wild* cherries, a half a mile from any house, and of course the owner considers them common property. I have got cherries there a number of times."

"That is no evidence you didn't steal them," said Nat, half laughing.

"If you do no worse stealing than that," answered John, "you will not be sent to jail this week."

It was therefore agreed, that the cherry-tree should be visited, even if they allowed the cherries to remain unmolested. Without further discussion they proceeded to execute their purpose, and lost no time in finding the famous tree. John's glowing description of the crop had caused their mouths to water long before they came in sight of them.

"John is hoaxing us," said Nat, smiling, before they were half way there. "I don't believe as good cherries as he tells about ever grow wild."

"Wait and see," responded John. "If you won't believe *me*, I guess you will your eyes. Wild or not wild, I hardly think you will keep your hands off, when you have a peak at them."

"I tell you what it is, Nat," said Frank, "if it should turn out that the cherries are tame, you might not get off so easy as Harry and Tom did for disturbing the exhibition."

"I shouldn't deserve to," answered Nat.

The conversation kept up briskly as the boys crossed the fields and scaled the walls and fences. At length they came in sight of the tree, standing apart from any garden, nursery, or orchard, a full half mile from the nearest house.

"There it is," said John, pointing to it. "If that is not a wild cherry-tree, then *no* tree is wild."

"I should think it would be as wild as the beasts, so far from any house," added Frank.

They were surprised, on approaching the tree, to find it loaded with cherries of so nice a quality. They were much larger than the common wild cherries, a sort of "mazards," similar to the kind that is cultivated in gardens.

"That is not a wild-cherry tree, I know," said Charlie. "It may have come up here, but the owner of this land would never fail to gather such cherries as these. They would sell for ninepence a quart in the village as quick as any cherries."

"I think so too," said Nat; "and if we strip the tree, the first thing we shall know, the constable will have us up for stealing."

"Pshaw!" exclaimed John. "You are more scared than hurt. I don't mean that these cherries are not like some that grow in gardens; but the tree came up here of itself—nobody ever set it out—and so it is wild; and why are not the cherries common property as much as that smaller kind which people get over there by the river?"

This last argument of John was more convincing. All the boys knew that anybody gathered the common wild cherries from trees that grew much nearer dwelling-houses than this, so that there was some force in John's last suggestion.

"If John *is* right," added Nat, "it is best to be on the safe side, and ask leave of the owner. If he does not mean to pick the cherries, he will be willing that we should have them; and if he does want them, he will put us into the lock-up for stealing them."

"Who is going half a mile to find the owner?" said John, "and then perhaps he will be away from home. I shall not run my legs off upon any such Tom Fool's errand. If you are a mind to do it, I have no objections, and I will pick the cherries while you are gone."

The matter was discussed a little longer, and finally all concluded to try the cherries. It required a pretty forcible argument to stand against the appeal of the luscious fruit to their eyes. Into the tree they went, and, in due time filled their caps with the tempting fruit. Having loaded their caps, they descended and set them on the ground under the tree, and then returned to fill their stomachs.

"Hark!" said Frank hurriedly, "do I not hear some one calling?"

"Yes," answered John, from the top of the tree, where he was regaling himself with the dessert, "true as I am alive, there is the owner coming full speed, and yelling like a good one. Let us clear."

They all dropped upon the ground instantly, and bounded over the nearest wall like frightened sheep, and soon were seen scampering a hundred rods off.

"There, now, if that isn't smart," exclaimed Nat; "we've left our caps under the tree, Frank."

John set to laughing to see the two capless boys; and he was more inclined to laugh because Charlie and himself had presence of mind enough to take theirs.

"If it was you, John, I shouldn't care a snap," said Frank. "You led the way, and made us believe that they were wild cherries, and I wish your cap was there."

John could only laugh, in reply, at his bareheaded companions.

"I don't see why we should run at all," said Nat, just apprehending the folly of their course. "We are not thieves,—we didn't mean to steal. We shouldn't have taken the cherries if we had known, the owner wanted them."

"What can we do without our hats?" asked Frank.

"I shall go and get mine," answered Nat, "and tell the man just as it was, and, if he is reasonable he will overlook it."

"I am beat now," exclaimed John; "the old fellow is certainly carrying off your caps."

The boys looked, and to their amazement, the man was returning to his house with the caps. Nat and Frank were more perplexed than ever.

"Never mind," said John; "you are both big enough to go bareheaded. What will you take for your caps?" and again he laughed at their predicament.

"What shall we do?" inquired Frank.

"Go to his house and get the caps, of course," said Nat. "The caps won't come to us that is certain."

"What will you tell the man?"

"Tell him the truth," replied Nat, "and it ought to get our caps, and shield us from punishment."

"Perhaps he is a crabbed fellow who will show us no favors; and he will say that our running away is evidence of our guilt."

"We were fools to run," said Nat; "and if I had stopped to think one moment I should have stayed there, and explained it to him."

Finally, it was decided that Nat and Frank should go after their caps, on which errand they started at once, while John and Charlie proceeded homeward. In the mean time the owner of the tree had reached his house very much amused at the flight of the capless boys. He was somewhat angry when he first saw the boys in his tree, but the possession of the two caps well filled with cherries modified his wrath considerably. It would take him two hours to pick that quantity of fruit. "Surely," he thought, "the boys have beaten the bush and I have caught the birds."

"You must go to the door and explain it," said Frank to Nat.

"I am going to, and convince him that we did did not mean to steal."

Nat gave a gentle rap at the door, to which a lady at once responded.

"Can we see the man who has our caps?" inquired Nat.

"I will see," she replied very kindly, and stepped back into the house to call her husband. He made his appearance promptly; and looked so much more pleasant than Nat expected, that he was very much emboldened.

"What is wanted, boys?" he asked.

"We have come," replied Nat, "to tell how it happened that we got your cherries, and to get our caps."

"I suppose it happened very much as it does every year with those cherries," said the man,—"the boys steal them."

"No, sir; I think I can convince you that we did not mean to steal. We thought they were wild cherries. John came along and told us about them, and we did not believe they were wild. Finally we consented to go and see, and when we got to the tree, we told him that the owner of such nice cherries would want them, and I told him that the best way would be to come and ask you, for if you did not want them, you would certainly give us permission to pick them. But he laughed at us, and said the tree was much further from any house than the wild cherries that any person gets down by the river, and therefore the cherries must be common property. We thought he was right, when he told us this, and so we went up into the tree."

"But why did you run when you saw me coming, if you did not mean to steal them?" he asked.

"I run, sir, because I did not stop to think. I told Frank, as soon as we stopped running, that we were very foolish, because we did not mean to steal, and I was sorry that we did run. But we were so surprised when we saw you coming that we ran before we thought. I don't think we did right, sir, though we did not mean to steal. It would have been better for us to have come and asked you for the cherries as I told John. Now we would like our caps, but we want you to be convinced first that we are not thieves."

"I *am* convinced," replied the man. "I guess you mean to be honest boys, and you shall have your caps."

The fact was, the man was much impressed with the sincerity and honesty of Nat before he got half through his explanation. He admired his frankness, and his manly, straight-forward way of telling his story. He went into the house and brought out the caps, just as he took them from the ground, full of cherries, and gave them caps, cherries, and all.

"You don't mean we shall have the cherries, do you?" inquired Nat.

"Certainly, you have worked hard enough for them," he replied. "And I like to see boys willing to own up when they do wrong. I don't think *you* meant to do wrong; but I am glad to see you make a clean breast of it, and not be so mean as to equivocate, and lie, to get out of a scrape. Boys always fare the best when they are truthful, and try to do right."

"We are much obliged to you," said Nat. "You will never catch us on your cherry-tree again without permission."

Having pocketed the cherries, they put on their caps, and hastened home, quite thoroughly convinced that all cherries which grow a half mile from any house are not wild.

CHAPTER V.

ATHLETIC SPORTS.

"A swim to-night," shouted John to Frank, on his way home from school. "All hands be there."

"Will you come, Nat?" inquired Frank.

"Yes; and swim three rods under water," was Nat's reply.

At this period of Nat's boyhood, there was almost a passion among the boys for athletic sports, such as swimming, jumping, running, ball-playing, and kindred amusements. For some time they had received special attention, and no one of the boys enjoyed them more than Nat. It was one of the principles on which he lived, to do with all his heart whatever he undertook. In the school-room, he studied with a keen relish for knowledge, and on the play- ground he played with equal gusto. If he had work to do it was attended to at once, and thoroughly finished in the shortest possible time. In this way he engaged in athletic sports.

An hour before sunset, a dozen or more boys were at "the bathing place."

"Now, Nat, for your three rods under water," said Frank. "If I was half as long-winded as you are, I should keep company with the fishes pretty often."

"He swam more than three rods under water the other day," said Charlie. "I shouldn't want to risk myself so long out of sight. Suppose the cramp should seize you, Nat, I guess you'd like to see the dry land."

"You must remember," suggested John, who was usually ready to turn things over, and look at the funny side, "that doctors won't wade into the water after their patients."

One after another the boys plunged into the water, as if it were their native element. Most of them had practised swimming, diving, and other feats, until they were adepts in these water-arts. Some of them could swim a surprising distance, and feared not to venture a long way from the shore. Frank was very skilful in performing these water feats, but even he could not equal Nat.

"Now for a swim under water," exclaimed Nat, as he disappeared from the view of his companions. All stopped their sports to watch Nat, and see where he would make his appearance. Not a word was spoken as they gazed with breathless interest, and waited to see him rise.

"He's drowned," cried one of the boys.

"No, no," responded Frank. "We shall see him in a moment," and yet Frank began to fear.

"I tell you he *is* drowned," shouted John, much excited. By this time there was a good deal of consternation among the boys, and some of them were running out of the water. A man who was watching on the shore, was actually stripping his coat off to make a plunge for Nat, when up he came.

"He is safe," shouted half a dozen voices, and the welkin rang with cheer after cheer.

"There, young man, better not try that again," said the gentleman on the shore, as Nat swum around in that direction.

"That was more than three rods," said Frank.

"And more than four," added Charlie. "You beat yourself this time, Nat. You never swam so far under water before. We thought you were drowned."

"There is no use in trying to beat *you*," continued Frank. "If you had gills you would be a regular fish."

Everybody in the village heard of Nat's swimming feats under water, as well as on the water, and it was not unusual for spectators to assemble on the shore, when they knew that he was going to bathe.

Not far from this time, a little later in the year perhaps, there was to be a special game of ball on Saturday afternoon. Ball-playing was one of the favorite games with the boys, and some of them were remarkable players. When the time arrived it was decided that John and Charlie should choose sides, and it fell to the latter to make the first choice.

"I choose Nat," said he.

"I'll take Frank," said John.

It was usually the case that Nat and Frank were pitted against each other in this amusement. Nat was considered the best player, so that he was usually the first choice. Frank stood next, so that he was the second choice. In this way they generally found themselves playing against each other. It was so on this occasion.

The game commenced, and John's side had the "ins."

"You must catch," said Charlie to Nat. It was usually Nat's part to catch.

"And you must throw," responded Nat. "I can catch your balls best."

The very first ball that was thrown, John missed, though he struck with a well-aimed blow, as he thought, and Nat caught it.

"That is too bad," was the exclamation heard on one side, and "good," "capital," on the other.

Charlie took the bat, and was fortunate in hitting the ball the first time he struck. Now it was Nat's turn, and, with bat in hand, he took his place.

"Be sure and hit," said Charlie.

"I should like to see a ball go by *him* without getting a rap," answered Frank, who was now the catcher. "The ball always seems to think it is no use to try to pass him."

"There, take that," said Nat, as he sent the ball, at his first bat, over the heads of all, so far that he had time to run round the whole circle of goals, turning a somerset as he came in.

"A good beginning, Nat; let us see you do that again," said Frank.

"When the time comes I'll give you a chance," replied Nat.

We will not follow the game further, but simply say that, before it was half through, quite a number of men, old and young, were attracted to the place by the sport.

"What a fine player for so young a boy," said one bystander to another, as Nat added one after another to the tallies.

"Yes; no one can excel him; he never plays second fiddle to anybody. He will run faster, catch better, and hit the ball more times in ten, than any other boy. I saw him jump the other day, and he surpassed any thing I have seen of his age."

"If that is not all he is good for, it is well enough," replied the other.

"He is just as good at studying or working, as he is at playing ball; it seems to be a principle with him *to be the best* in whatever he undertakes. I was amused at his reply to one of the neighbors, who asked him how he managed to swim better than any one else. 'It is just as easy to swim well as poorly,' said he, and there is a good deal of truth in the remark. At another time he said, 'one might as well run fast as slow.'"

"Does he appear to glory in his feats?"

"Not at all. He does not seem to think there is much credit in being the best at these games. One of the boys said to him one day, 'Nat, you always get all the glory in our games.' He replied, 'I don't think there is much glory in playing ball well. If that is all a person is good for, he is not good for much.' He has very good ideas about such things."

This was really a correct view of Nat's case. He enjoyed athletic sports as much as any of the boys, and yet he actually felt that it was no particular credit to him to be a good swimmer, jumper, runner, or ball-player. He did not study to excel therein because he thought it was honorable to beat every other boy in these things. But what he did, he did with all his soul, and this is necessary to success. He had confidence in his ability to succeed in what he undertook. When he first went into the water, he knew he could learn to swim. When he took his stand to catch the ball, he knew he could catch it. Others did these things, and he could see no reason why he could not. He seemed to feel as one of the Rothschilds did, who said, "I can do what another man can." The same elements of character caused him to excel on the play- ground, that enabled him to bear off the palm in the school-room.

It is generally the case that a boy who does one thing well will do another well also. Employers understand this, and choose those lads who exhibit a disposition to be thorough. Said Samuel Budgett, "In whatever calling a man is found, he ought to be the best in his calling; if only a shoe-black, he ought to be the best shoe-black in the neighborhood." He acted upon this principle himself from his boyhood; and so did Nat, whether he was fully conscious of it or not. Sir Joshua Reynolds, the great painter, said that his success resulted mainly from one principle upon which he had acted, namely, *to make every picture the best.*

Buxton, of whom we have spoken already, had as much force of character in his youth as almost any boy who ever lived. His determination was invincible, and his energy and perseverance were equal to his resolution. The consequence was that he became famous for boating, shooting, riding, and all sorts of fieldsports, though he cared little for any thing else. But when, at last, his attention was turned to self-improvement and philanthropy, by the influence of the Gurney family, he carried the same qualities with him there, and through them won a world-wide fame. It was thus with Sir Walter Scott, who was second to no one in his youth for his dexterity and proficiency in athletic, games, and the various forms of recreation. He could "spear a salmon with the best fisher on the Tweed, and ride a wild horse with any hunter in Yarrow." The same energy and unconquerable will helped him achieve that herculean labor afterwards, of paying off a debt of six hundred thousand dollars, with his pen. The Duke of Wellington acknowledged the same principle, when he said, as he stood watching the sports of boys on the play- ground of Eton, where he spent his juvenile years, "It was there that the battle of Waterloo was won."

Twenty-five years after Nat bore off the palm in athletic games, an early associate asked him to what he owed his success, and he answered, in a vein of pleasantry, "To swimming under water." Whatever may have been his meaning, it is not at all difficult to discover the same elements of character in squash-raising, declamation, and arithmetic, that appear in the games he played.

His skill in the water served him a good purpose one day, or rather, it served another boy well. Nat and two or three of his companions were at play near the factory, when some one cried out, "A boy in the water!"

In an instant Nat sprung, followed by his companions, and made for the water, when lo! a little boy was seen struggling to keep from sinking. He had carelessly ventured too near and fallen in, and must have perished but for the timely aid thus rendered him. Nat plunged in after him, and his play-fellows did the same, or brought rails, by which he was saved. He proved to be Charlie's younger brother.

This event made a deep impression upon Nat's mind, and he reflected upon his act with far more satisfaction than he did upon his superiority in swimming or playing ball. He had saved, or helped save, a lad from a watery grave, and that was an act worth performing. He went home, and after relating the incident with the greatest enthusiasm, he sat down and drew a picture representing the scene. There was the water and buildings near, a little boy struggling for life, and Nat and associates plunging in after him. It was really a good representation of the terrific scene; and Nat considered it quite an accession to his collection of drawings. Thus he used this bit of experience to advance himself in one branch of education. With his traits of character, he could not excel in innocent games, without receiving an impulse therefrom to excel in more important acquisitions.

CHAPTER VI.

A MISTAKE.

Stern Winter locked the streams again. A snowy mantle covered the hills and valleys, and the bleak winds moaned through the naked trees. The merry sleigh-bells jingled in the streets, and merrier lads and lasses filled the village school-house. The skating grounds never presented more attractions to Nat and his circle of schoolmates.

"The ice is smooth as glass," said John. "I never saw better skating in my life. Will you try it right after school?"

These words were addressed to a group of school-boys at the afternoon recess, to which all but two responded in the affirmative. It was a snapping cold day, but youthful skaters mind nothing for that.

"George and I have promised to see the teacher after school about studying grammar," said Neander, "so that we can't go."

"He wants to form a new class in grammar for beginners, and our parents have told him that we must study it," said George.

"I will sell you what *I* know about it cheap, if you will go with us," said John, who had studied grammar a short time.

"I don't think he will be troubled to find use for as much as that," said Charlie, jocosely.

"You will find it dry as a chip," added John. "It fairly makes me thirsty to study it."

The bell rung, and the boys hurried to their seats. At the close of the school, the teacher took occasion to say, "that some scholars were desirous of beginning the study of grammar. I think there might be quite a large class formed of those who are old enough to begin. It is a very important science. It will teach you how to read and write the English language correctly. You cannot write a good letter even without some knowledge of this study. Those of you who are eleven or twelve years of age ought to commence it at once. Now, those of you who would like to join such a class may stop after the school is dismissed, and we will make the arrangements."

Three or four only remained—others passed out, Nat and Charlie among them. They had never studied grammar, and the teacher really expected they would remain. Their scholarship was so good that he inferred they would desire to unite with such a class, but he was mistaken.

"Shall you join the grammar class, Nat?" inquired Charlie, on their way to the pond.

"No; I think that other studies will be of more use to me. Grammar is a good branch for rich men's sons, who can go to school as long as they want to; but I am not a rich man's son, and I never expect to do any thing that will require a knowledge of grammar."

"That is my idea exactly," continued Charlie. "If I knew I should ever go into a store, or be a town officer, I should want to study it."

"According to the teacher's ideas, you will need it if you are nothing more than a wood-sawyer's clerk," said John.

"I didn't quite believe all the teacher said about writing letters," added Nat. "I have heard father say that grammar was not studied at all when *he* went to school, and that it has been introduced into school quite recently. Now I would like to know if people did not understand how to write letters in those days. Couldn't Washington and Jefferson, and other great men, write letters correctly?"

"I never thought of that," said Charlie. "I would ask the teacher, if I were in your place, to-morrow."

"For one," said John, "I should be willing to run my risk, if I could get rid of studying it. I can't make much out of it."

"I have no doubt," added Nat, "that it is a good study for those who will want to use it; but *I*(?) shall never want to use it, and it is better for me to study something else. Arithmetic is useful to everybody, if they never buy any thing but meat out of a butcher's cart."

By this time they had reached the pond, so that the subject of grammar was dropped, and skating taken up.

"I suppose you will bear off the palm as usual, Nat," said Frank, while he was putting on his skates.

"I don't know about that," replied Nat; "if a fellow can't skate some on this glare ice, he better give his skates to somebody who can."

Frank's remark was drawn out by the fact that Nat was already considered the best skater in the village. He could skate more rapidly, and perform more feats on his skates than any one else. His ability had been fully tested again and again; and by this time there seemed to be a sort of expectation among the boys that he would be "first best" in whatever he undertook. For this reason they hardly attempted to compete with him, but yielded the first place to him as a matter of course.

Away went Nat up the pond, and Charlie exclaimed,

"See him go! What a fellow Nat is! any thing he undertakes has to go. See him skate now on one foot, and now he is skating backwards!"

"And he does it just as easy as a boy knows his father," said John.

For nearly an hour skating was enjoyed, when all concluded that their suppers would be waiting, and so they separated for home.

On the following day, soon after school began in the morning, the teacher brought up the subject of a grammar class, evidently dissatisfied that certain boys did not remain after school, on the previous afternoon, to join it. He remarked "that there were several boys in school, who might study grammar as well as not," and he went on to call the names of some, and turning to Nat and Charlie, who sat together, he said, "Both of you need to begin this study at once. It would have been better if you had undertaken it before; but it is not too late now. You will never regret it hereafter. I want both of you to join the class," and he uttered the last sentence as if he meant it.

Neither Nat nor Charlie made any reply at the time; but at recess they went to the teacher and made known their feelings.

"We never expect to do any thing that will require a knowledge of grammar," said Nat. "It will do well enough for rich men's sons."

"Perhaps both of you will be lawyers, ministers, legislators, or governors yet," replied the teacher, smiling. "Poorer boys than you have risen to occupy as important places, and the like may happen again."

"None of the scholars like grammar," said Charlie; "they say it is dry and uninteresting, and hard to understand."

"If it is so," answered the teacher, "that is no reason why it should not be studied. We have to do some very unpleasant things in this world. If you live to become men, you will find that you cannot have every thing to your taste. You will be obliged to do some things, from the doing of which you would rather be excused. And as to your not expecting to occupy stations in future life, where you will find a knowledge of grammar useful, there is more prospect of it than there was that Benjamin Franklin would become distinguished. He had not half so good advantages as you have. His father was poor, and had a large family to support. He was compelled to take Benjamin out of school, when ten years old, and set him to making soap, which was not very popular business. But the boy did as well as he could, and made improvement though deprived of school advantages. Then he became a printer boy, and used all his spare moments to read and study, so that he advanced more rapidly than many of his companions did who continued in school. He always had to work, and had much more reason than you have, when he was of your age, to say that he should never occupy a position of influence. Yet he became, as you know, one of the most learned men of his age, a philosopher and statesman whose fame will never perish. And it was somewhat so with Patrick Henry. Though he had better advantages than Benjamin Franklin, and had a father who was able to assist him, yet no one thought he would ever become distinguished. It was rather thought by the people who knew him, that he would never accomplish much. Yet, when he came to improve the small opportunities he had, after his father had ceased to aid him, he rapidly advanced to fame. He became the most noted orator of his day, and a very popular statesman. When he was twelve years old, he had no idea of occupying such a place in manhood. He would have laughed at the suggestion. There are many such examples; and they show us that boys may rise to stations they never expect to hold, so that your plea for not studying grammar is a poor one. At any rate, both of you will have occasion to write letters, and perhaps you will be a town clerk or justice. I shall insist upon your studying grammar."

Nat and Charlie exchanged glances, as the teacher rung the bell for the boys to come in. They saw that it was no use to hold out against his wishes, for his last remark had settled the matter. Therefore they reluctantly yielded to his request.

This was the first instance in which Nat had exhibited any unwillingness to take up a new study. But he had made up his mind that it would not be of any use to him, so that he had little heart for the science. He commenced it, and recited his lessons, though rather mechanically, without clearly understanding them, at the same time excelling in arithmetic, declamation, and other exercises that engaged his attention. As his school days ended a few months after, his knowledge of grammar was very limited indeed. The sequel will disclose whether he was not finally convinced that the teacher was right, while he himself was wrong, and whether the failure to improve even one small opportunity does not become the occasion of future regret.

"Well, Nat, how do you like grammar?" inquired John, some weeks afterwards.

"As well as I can," replied Nat.

"So do I, and that isn't saying much. But I thought you was determined not to study it."

"I thought so too," replied Nat, "and you see what thought did."

"I suppose you concluded that you would want to write letters to your sweetheart some time, and it would be a pity not to use the English language with propriety in such a case."

"I didn't think much about it; but when a boy can't do as he likes, there is no way left but to do as he must, and that is my case."

"I thought the teacher bore rather hard upon us," said Charlie, who had been listening to the conversation.

"Perhaps you will thank him for it when you get to be Dr. Franklin, Jr.," answered Nat, in a jesting manner.

"It can't be denied," interrupted John, "that the teacher is a great grammarian. Didn't he put Sam into the objective case yesterday, when he tumbled him head over heels out of his seat? If his action didn't pass over to an object then, I won't guess again."

"Sam looked as if he was convinced that the teacher was an active verb," said Nat. "He found out that he was neither neuter nor passive."

The subject of grammar became a frequent theme of remark during the remainder of the term among the boys. None of them liked it very well, so that poor grammar was slandered, and many a joke was cracked over it.

It was during this term that Sam Drake allowed his mischief-making propensity to exhibit itself in a cruel act, for which he was condemned by nearly all beholders. The boys were returning from school one night, when a well-known dog, belonging to a neighbor, came out to salute his young master, one of the scholars. He was somewhat larger than Trip, and a playful fellow, ready to frolic with the boys.

"Come here, Spot," said Sam to the dog, "good fellow, can you run after a stick to-night?" and he patted him upon his head, till the dog (who was usually shy of Sam) seemed to think that he was a good friend. "There, go and bring that to me," at the same time throwing a little stick one or two rods.

Spot obeyed at once, and brought back the stick, apparently conscious of having performed his duty well.

"What do you suppose he would do if I should tie my dinner pail to his tail?" inquired Sam.

"You shan't do it," cried two or three boys, none more loudly, however, than Nat.

"I *shall* do it, if I am a mind to," replied Sam; and he proceeded to take a string out of his pocket for this purpose.

"You are too bad to do that," said John, trying to dissuade him from doing it.

"It seems to me that you all have a heap of pity just now," said Sam.

"I wish *you* had," responded Nat.

"*You* would get precious little of it, Mr. Squash-peddler, if I had," answered Sam. "The dog is none of your relations, and you needn't trouble yourself about him."

Ben Drake, ere this, had turned to aid Sam in executing his purpose, and the pail was actually tied to Spot's tail before this conversation closed.

"Take off the cover," said Ben, and no quicker said than done; whereupon Spot ran yelping down the street, the tin pail rattling behind him so as to frighten him beyond measure. The faster he ran, the more the pail rattled, and the more terrified the dog was. Men stopped in the street to see the cruel sport, and express their disapproval.

"It is one of Sam Drake's tricks," said Charlie to an inquiry put by a gentleman.

Sam and Ben laughed till they could scarcely stand upon their feet to see the dog run. It was just such sport as they loved.

"Hurrah for Spot!" shouted Sam, swinging his hat. "He'll spill his dinner if he don't carry the pail more carefully."

"If it was *my* dog," said Frank, "you would find my father after you."

"You ought to be ashamed of yourself," added Nat. "It would not have been more cruel in you to kill him outright. You are always up to something of the kind."

Not one of the boys approved of Sam's and Ben's cruelty. All expressed decided sympathy for Spot, and were glad to see the pail drop from his tail by the time he had run thirty or forty rods.

"What kind of a noun is Sam?" inquired John, with one of his roguish glances of the eye.

"A proper noun, of course," replied Charlie.

"Not by any means," said Nat; "it takes a decent fellow to be a *proper* noun. Sam is an *im*-proper noun. I don't believe he has behaved *proper* one whole day in five years."

This remark got a hearty laugh upon Sam, and he felt it. He mumbled over something, and shook his fist a little, but Nat could hear no part of his remark but the oath that closed it. Sam was very profane, and his brother was too. It was not unusual for both of them to utter the most wicked oaths. They seemed to delight in using the worst words of the English language.

This barbarous act of Sam was frequently spoken of thereafter, and he stood lower than ever in the estimation of Nat. The latter possessed tender feelings towards all sorts of animals, and he was much disposed to pet them. It might be almost said of him as Parry did of Sir John Franklin, "he never turned his back upon a danger, yet he was so tender that he would not brush away a mosquito."

The winter session of the school closed, and vacation brought its work and pleasures. We should be glad to follow Nat through these few weeks of vacation, but we must hasten to a scene that was enacted when the following summer was far spent.

CHAPTER VII.

PROSPECT HILL.

"Nat," said Frank, as they were going home from school one Friday night of the following summer, "let us go up on Prospect Hill to-morrow afternoon; it will be a capital time for a view, if it is a clear day."

"Agreed," responded Nat. "I told Harry the other day that I could count a hundred churches from that hill, and he laughed at me, and I mean to see if I was far from the truth."

"Well, I guess you set it a little too high," said Frank, "but it is a grand sight that we have there."

"Yes! I heard Mr. Sawtelle (Nat's pastor) say, that he never enjoyed such a fine prospect anywhere else, because so many different objects can be seen. I wish I could look through a spy-glass from that hill, wouldn't it be fine?"

Just then the two boys reached a corner where they must separate to go to their respective homes, and the engagement was renewed by Nat's saying, "Now remember, Frank, and be along in good season."

A word about Prospect Hill. We are not sure that this was the veritable name given to this lofty eminence at that time; but we call it thus now because we have heard Nat designate it thus since he became a man. It is certainly a very appropriate appellation with which to christen a hill that towers up so abruptly toward heaven.

This hill was situated just back of Nat's native village, perhaps a half mile or more from the common on which he was wont to play. The top of it was crowned with a mammoth rock, which an enthusiastic geologist might call its crown jewel. Indeed, we are inclined to believe that nearly the whole hill is composed of granite, from base to top, and were the rocky eminence near some "Giants' Causeway," we should regard it the work of these fabled characters, perhaps begun as the first rough stepping stone to the stars.

The boys were right when they spoke so earnestly of the grand view presented from the brow of this hill. There was nothing like it in all the "region round about;" and it is grander still at the present day, because the cunning hand of art has beautified almost every foot of land in view, and reared structures of varied form and costliness on every hand. In the magnificent panorama appear a score of little villages nestling among the distant trees, while as many larger ones stand forth in more imposing grandeur, and several cities spread out their wealth of stores and palaces, and lift their church spires and domes of public edifices high to the blazing sun. Dame Nature lends enchantment to the view by the freshness and beauty of her inimitable landscape. Green and mossy meadow, rich, cultivated upland, luxurious gardens, sweet shady grottos and cozy dells, orchards, forests, farms, with almost every variety of natural scenery, enliven the prospect beyond description; and last, though not least of all, a beautiful river pursues its serpentine course through dusky everglades and grass-grown valleys, as if an unearthed mine, fused by subterranean fires, were pouring forth its vast treasures in a stream of molten silver. The scene is so truly grand that neither tongue nor pen can do justice to the reality.

Saturday afternoon came as usual, with its freedom from school-hour quiet and study. Frank was on time, accompanied by his knowing little dog, "Trip," and Nat was as much on time as he.

"Halloo! Frank," exclaimed Nat; "going to take Trip along with us?"

"Yes! he'll enjoy it as well as we," replied Frank.

"And *I* shall enjoy it a good deal better to have him with us," continued Nat. "Come here Trip, you nice little fellow, and see the best friend you have." And Trip bounded upon him, giving him as hearty a "good afternoon" as a dog can, while Nat returned the compliment by patting him upon his neck, and telling him, as he glanced a curious eye at Frank, "that he knew almost as much as his master."

"I wish that dog was mine," said Nat.

"*I* don't," responded Frank; "but I wish you had one just like him."

"I suppose you don't know where I can buy his brother or sister, do you?"

Frank smiled, and before he had time to reply, they were hailed by Sam and Ben Drake.

"Where now, boys?" inquired Sam.

"Bound for Prospect Hill: it is a good clear day for a fine view, and I am going to count the churches," answered Nat.

"Count your grandmothers!" sneeringly exclaimed Sam. "I would give more to roll a big stone down the steep side than I would for the best view you can get from the top."

"But don't you think the prospect from the hill is fine, Sam?"

"Fine enough, I s'pose, though I don't know much about it, as I never thought it was best to injure my eyes looking."

"Well, I must say that you——"

"There, take that, you little whelp," just then shouted Sam to Trip, as he gave the little dog a kick that sent him half across the road.

It seems that Trip happened to come in Sam's way, so that he stumbled against him, and this aroused his ire at once, and then followed the cruel assault. The dog certainly did not mean to come in his way, for he was not a boy that even the dogs liked. They usually kept a respectable distance from both Sam and Ben, and saved their good-will for such kind boys as Nat and Frank. Dogs learn very readily who their friends are, and they wag their tails and skip around those only who are.

Frank looked at Nat when he saw his favorite dog thus abused, and the glance which they exchanged told what each of them thought of the barbarous treatment. Nothing was said, however, and they passed on. It was evident, by this time, that Sam and his brother intended to accompany them, without an invitation, to Prospect Hill. While they are on the way, we will improve the time to say a word about Nat's love of nature.

Sam could see no beauty in a landscape. Why any person should want to stand upon a hill-top for a whole half hour to view green lawns, gardens, meadows, and villages and cities, with their church spires and domes, he could not understand, especially after they had seen them once. If he could have been put into Eden, it would have been no sport for him, unless he could have had the privilege of clubbing the cats and stoning the dogs.

It was different with Nat. He never tired of the view from Prospect Hill, and this love of nature and art contributed to elevate his character. This is always the case. Scarcely any person has become renowned for learning, in whom this love was not early developed. Sir Francis Chantrey was one of the most distinguished artists of his day, possessing a nice discrimination and a most delicate taste, to aid him in his remarkable imitations of nature. He was reared upon a farm, where he enjoyed the innocent pleasure of ranging the forests, climbing hills, bathing in ponds and streams, and rambling through vale and meadow for fowl and fish, all of which he did with a "relish keen." Perhaps he owed more to the inspiration of the wild scenes of Derby Hills, than to all the books that occupied his attention in his boyhood's days. The same was true of the gifted poet Burns, whose sweet and lofty verse has made the name of Scotland, his native land, immortal. He took his first lessons from the green fields, and gushing bird-songs, on his father's farm. Silently, and unconsciously to himself, dame Nature waked his poetic genius into life, when he followed the plough, angled in his favorite stream, or played "echo" with the neighboring woods. The late Hugh Miller, also, the world-renowned geologist, might have been unknown to fame but for the unconscious tuition that he derived from the rocky sides of Cromarty Hill, and his boyish exploration of Doocot Caves. He loved nature more than he loved art. There was nothing that suited him better than to be scaling the rugged sides of hills, exploring deep, dark caverns, and hunting shells and stones on the sea-shore. He was naturally rough, headstrong, and heedless—qualities that tend to drag a youth down to ruin. But his love of nature opened a path of innocent thought and amusement before him, and saved him from a wretched life.

Thus the facts of history show that there is more hope of a boy who loves the beautiful in nature and art, than of him who, like Sam Drake, cared for neither. Perhaps we shall learn that it would have been better for Sam if he had thought more favorably of nature, and less of rude and cruel sports.

The boys reached the top of the hill before two o'clock. Sam Drake was the first to set his foot upon its solid apex, and he signalized the event by swinging his hat, and shouting,

"Three cheers for the meeting-houses!"

This was done, of course, as a sort of reflection upon Nat, who made no reply. Sam was about three years older than Nat, and yet Nat was the most of a man.

"A fire in Boston," exclaimed Frank, as soon as he reached the summit, and cast his eyes towards the city. All looked, and, to their surprise, there was a dense volume of smoke issuing from the north part of the city, indicating that a terrific fire was raging. Had it been in the night-time, the whole heavens would have been lighted up with the blaze, and the scene would have been grand beyond description. But in the sunlight, nothing but smoke could be seen.

"What do you suppose it is burning?" inquired Frank. "It must be some large building, I should think by the smoke it makes. Perhaps it is a whole block on fire."

"I guess it is one of Nat's churches," said Sam, casting a glance at the person hit by the remark. "He had better count it before it is gone."

"Well," replied Nat, who was tempted by the last fling to answer, "I know of one fellow——"

And there he stopped short, for his caution prevailed, and he concluded that "the least said the better." He had a pretty cutting remark on the tip of his tongue, when he remembered that Sam was older than himself, and was base enough to return a blow for a word. Besides, he had a special dislike for Sam, since his cruel treatment of Spot, which would naturally lead him to say as little to him as possible.

"What is that you know about a fellow?" said Sam, growing angry. "It is a lucky thing for you that you didn't say it. Give me any of your sarce, and I'll let you know who is the oldest. Boys that count churches better look two ways for Sunday."

Frank saw how things were going, so he sought to quell the storm in Sam's breast by calling the attention of all to the peculiar symmetry and beauty of an elm tree that stood in the distance. But Sam, not caring to view such objects, turned away to hurl stones, with which he had taken care to fill his pockets, at some object near the base of the hill. Frank's device, however, accomplished the object intended.

"How many miles do you think we can see from the top of this hill?" inquired Nat, addressing himself to Frank.

"Well, I hardly know," answered Frank. "We can see Boston very plainly, and that is ten miles distant. We can see further still in the other direction, perhaps twice as far."

"How fine this is!" continued Nat. "But I must begin to count the churches, or I shall not get through this afternoon. One, two, three, four, five, six, seven, eight, nine, ten—yes, here are ten right here within a few miles. And now let us count them——"

He was stopped here in the middle of a sentence, by the yelp of the dog Trip, and both turned to see what was the matter with him, when Sam shouted:

"Look here, Frank, dogs are falling. Trip has taken the shortest cut down hill this time."

"Good!" added Ben. "I wish all the dogs were kicked after him." And both Sam and Ben seemed to glory in the calamity that had befallen Trip.

Frank and Nat stood appalled when they saw what the trouble was. Sam had kicked Trip down the precipitous side of the hill, where there was a fearful plunge of thirty or forty feet; and there he lay motionless upon his side. Although they stood so far above the dog, it was very evident that he was dead. Frank burst into tears as the unwelcome truth flashed upon his mind that Trip was no more. It was a full, overflowing gush of grief from the bottom of his heart. Nat felt badly to see the dog killed, and also at seeing the grief into which Frank was plunged, and *he* began to weep also; and there the two boys cried as sincerely over the lifeless dog, as ever friend shed tears over the corpse of friend.

"Well done, now, if I ain't beat!" exclaimed Sam. "Crying over a dead dog! Better save your tears for his funeral, Frank. I'll preach his funeral sermon if you'll name a text. And you come in second mourner, do you, Nat?"

"Second mourner or not," answered Nat, wiping his eyes, and roused by the scene into a magnanimous self-defence, "if I was in Frank's place, your father should know of this."

"Well, 'spose he does know it, what do you think I care?" responded Sam. "I'd like to see the old man calling me to an account for killing a dog."

"So should I like to see him do it," quickly added Nat, "if he would give you what you deserve."

Ben evidently relented by this time for his harsh saying about the matter, and addressing his brother, he said,

"After all, Sam, I think it was rather too bad to kill Trip, for he was the cleverest dog in town. I don't think you'll gain many friends by the act."

"I didn't mean to kill him," said Sam.

"But you might have known that it *would* kill him to kick him down such a place as that," said Nat.

"That is not so clear, my boy," replied Sam; "it takes a boy bright enough to count meeting-houses to do that. You see I am green—it is the bright feller, who can speak pieces, and look at the fields and trees from Prospect Hill, to foresee such events."

"Come, Sam, you are a little too bad," said Ben. "I don't think you'd like it very well if Frank should kill your gray squirrel the first chance he has."

Sam found it difficult to argue the case with his brother Ben against him, who had really been converted over to the other side by the tears of Frank and Nat. Ben was always a better boy than Sam, but he often yielded to his wicked counsels because Sam was the eldest. Ben was made worse by his brother's influence. This was the general impression in the neighborhood. Sam also, owed a spite to good boys in general, who ranked higher than himself in school, and were thought more highly of in the community. He knew that Nat was a favorite, in school and out, with all who knew him, and so he was envious and vindictive. He twitted him about thinking more of himself than he ought, although he did not really think so. The fact was, Nat was far in advance of Sam in reading, writing, arithmetic, and every branch of study, although the latter was three years older. This circumstance probably excited the ill-will of Sam, as he had an evil disposition, made more evil every day by his vicious course. What he said and did on that day was the result of his jealousy and envy, in connection with his bad temper and reckless spirit. Probably he did not think of killing Trip, when he gave him a kick, for he was utterly reckless, and scarcely ever stopped to consider consequences. But this was no excuse. It is evidence rather of a more dangerous temper of mind.

Sam gave Ben a wink, and both hurried away together, leaving Nat and Frank alone, as they were glad to be.

"How cruel Sam is!" said Frank, breaking the silence that prevailed after they were left alone.

"Worse than that," added Nat. "I begin to think that what Mr. Bond said the other day about him will prove true."

"What *did* he say?"

"He said that Sam would become a very bad man, unless he turned his course soon, and that he should not be surprised if he came to the gallows. I thought at once of a story which I read the other day about a boy."

"Do you mean a boy like Sam?"

"Yes; very much like him. He lived in England, and he was neighbor to a minister there. The minister had two or three sons whom he warned not to associate with this bad boy. He told them that he would come to some bad end because he did not obey his parents, and was so wicked in other respects. And it proved true; for, in a few years he was shut up in prison for his crimes."

"Sam ought to be put there for what he has done already," said Frank. "But come, let us go round and get poor Trip's body. He shall have a decent burial at any rate."

Both started up, and hastened down the hill to a spot from which they might turn and pass round to where Trip lay. They were soon at his side. Frank took up his lifeless body, and the tears started afresh as he said, "stone dead."

"Oh, how sorry I am that we let Trip come with us!" said Nat.

"So am I, but it can't be helped now; his neck is broke, and neither of us can mend it."

"Let us carry him home as a witness against Sam. Your folks will want to see him once more, too, and I know that my father and mother would be glad to." Thus Nat expressed himself as they turned their steps homeward. Silently they walked on, Frank carrying the dog-corpse in his arms, as solemn as ever pall-bearer bore the remains of human being to the grave. We will leave them to get home in their own time, while we look in upon Nat's father and mother.

CHAPTER VIII.

THE END OF SCHOOL-DAYS.

In the course of the afternoon Nat's father met the agent of the factory, and the following conversation ensued:—

"What do you say about letting your boy come into the factory to work?" said the agent. "We are greatly in need of a boy to carry bobbins, and we will give him two dollars a week."

"I'll see what his mother says about it. I suppose he will have to do something for a living soon. I shall not be able to do much more for him."

"But Nat has worked some already in a factory, has he not?"

"Well, not exactly to make it a business. He was at his uncle's, in Lowell, about six months, and he was a 'picker boy' a short time."

"That is enough to initiate him. It is only a step from 'picker boy' to 'bobbin boy.'"

The facts about his going to Lowell were these: He had an uncle there who was a clergyman, and Nat was one of his favorites, as he was generally with all those who knew him intimately. This uncle proposed that Nat should come and stay with him a few months in the new "city of spindles" (for the city was then only about four years old), a sort of baby-city. The lad was only eleven years old, at that time, though he was more forward and manly than most boys are at fifteen. He was somewhat pleased with the idea of going to his uncle's, and engaged in preparing for the event with a light heart. As the time drew near for his departure, he found he loved home more than he thought he did, and he almost wished that he had not decided to go. But being a boy of much decision, as we have seen, he was rather ashamed to relinquish what he had undertaken to do. He said little or nothing therefore about his feelings, but went at the appointed time. Soon after he became a member of his uncle's family, where he was a very welcome visitor, a "picker boy" was wanted in the factory, and arrangements were made for Nat to fill the place. He entered upon the work, well pleased to be able to earn something for his parents, and he fully satisfied his employers, by his close attention to his work, his respectful manners, and his amiable, intelligent, and gentlemanly bearing. But Nat loved home too well to be contented to remain long away. He had seasons of being homesick, when he thought he would give more to see his father and mother again than for any thing beside. His uncle saw that the boy was really growing thin under the intense longing of his heart for home, so he wrote to his parents, and arrangements were made immediately for his return. It was a happy day for Nat when he reached home, and took his parents once more by the hand. Home never seemed more precious than it did then. If he had been a singer, I have no doubt that he would have made the old homestead resound with the familiar song of Payne,

"'Mid pleasures and palaces though we may roam,
Be it ever so humble, there's no place like home."

It is a good sign for boys to love home. Good boys always do love home. It is the place where their parents dwell, whom they love and respect. No ties are so dear as those which bind them to this sacred spot. No love is purer than that which unites them to parents, brothers, and sisters. It may be a home of poverty, where few of the comforts, and none of the luxuries of life are found, but this does not destroy its charm. Sickness and misfortune may be there, and still it is home, loved and sought. Others may have more splendid homes, where affluence gathers much to please the eye and fascinate the heart, but they would not be received in exchange for this.

Such boys as Sam and Ben Drake seldom love home. Disobedient and headstrong children do not love their parents much, and, for this reason, home has few charms except as a place to eat and sleep. The history of nearly all base men will show that in early life they broke away from the restraints of home, and ceased to love the place where parents would guide them in the path of virtue. Some years ago a distinguished philanthropist visited a young man about twenty-eight years of age, who was confined in prison for passing counterfeit money. His sentence was imprisonment for life. He had become very sad and penitent in consequence of his imprisonment, and the fact that consumption was rapidly carrying him to the grave. The philanthropist inquired into his history. When he spoke to the prisoner of his mother, he observed that his chin quivered, and that tears came unbidden to his eyes.

"Was not your mother a Christian?" inquired the visitor.

"Oh yes, sir!" he answered; "many and many a time has she warned me of this."

"Then you had good Christian parents and wholesome instruction at home, did you not?"

"Certainly; but it all avails me nothing now."

"Then why are you here?"

Raising himself up in bed to reply to this last inquiry, the young man said,

"I can answer you that question in a word. I did not obey my parents nor care for home." And he uttered these last words with a look and tone of despair that sent a chill through the interrogator's heart.

This is but one illustration of the truth, that boys who do not love home usually make shipwreck of their characters. Probably Sam Drake would have laughed at Nat, or any other boy, for being homesick, and said,

"I should like to see *myself* tied to mother's apron strings. It will do for babies to cry to see their mothers, but it will not do for men. Suppose it *is* home, there are other places in creation besides home. I'd have folks know that there's one feller who can go away from home, and stay too."

A great many men who are now in prison, or dishonored graves, talked exactly so when they were young. They thought it was manly to have their own way, and show that they cared little for home.

Nat's love of home, then, was a good omen. It was not a discredit to him to long to get back again to his father and mother. It was the evidence of an obedient, affectionate, amiable son.

After the conversation between the agent and Nat's father, the latter went home to consult his wife upon the subject. He related to her the substance of his conversation with the agent, and waited her reply.

"I hardly know what to say," said she. "Nat is only twelve years old, and needs all the schooling he can get. His teachers have said so much to me about his talents, and their wish that he might be educated, that I have hoped, and almost expected, some unforeseen way might be opened for his love of study to be gratified."

"That is entirely out of the question, I think," replied her husband. "The time has come, too, when he must earn something for his support. I see not how we can get along and keep him at school. He loves his books I know, and I should be very glad to see him enjoy them, but poor folks must do as they can and not as they want to."

"Very true; but it is so hard to think that his schooling must end here, when he is only a little boy. I don't know but it would break his heart to be told that he could go to school no more."

"He need not be told *that*," added her husband. "He may not know but that he will go to school again at some future day."

"It will be difficult to satisfy him on that point, if we keep honesty on our side. You are not with him so much as I am, so that you do not know how inquisitive he is, nor how much he talks about his books, and getting learning.

The first thing he will think of will be, whether he will go to school any more. He knows that factory boys are deprived of this privilege, and as he is to become a factory boy, his inference will be that there is no more schooling for him."

"Well, it must come to that, and he may as well know it first as last. But I do not apprehend that he will lay it seriously to heart, for he is always ready to do what his parents think is best. I think he is remarkable for that."

"I think so too; and I shall rely more upon his disposition in this respect to be reconciled to the privation of school, than upon any thing else. I think if the subject is brought before him at the right time, and in the right way, I can convince him it is for the best, and I am sure he will be ready to do what will be best for all of us."

The conclusion of the matter was that Nat should enter the factory on Monday, and that his mother should open the subject to him as soon as he came home.

CHAPTER IX.

OPENING THE SUBJECT.

The door suddenly opened, and in rushed Nat, under great excitement, with his eyes "as large as saucers," to use a hyperbole, which means only that his eyes looked very large indeed.

"Sam Drake has killed little Trip," said he to his mother.

"Killed Trip!" reiterated his mother, with great surprise.

"Yes; he kicked him down the steep side of Prospect Hill, and he is stone dead."

"What did he do that for? Had he any trouble with Frank?"

"No, mother; he did it because he is an ugly boy, and for nothing else. He is always doing some wrong thing. The teacher told him the other day that he had more difficulty with the scholars than all the other boys put together. Frank and I didn't want he should go with us; but he and Ben came along and went without being asked to go."

"They are very bad boys," added his mother, "and I am afraid they will make bad men. It is well known that they are disobedient at home, and cause their parents a great deal of trouble, Sam especially."

"And such swearers I never heard in my life," continued Nat. "Every third word Sam speaks is profane. And he is vulgar too. I wish you knew how bad he is."

"I hope you will avoid his company as much as possible. Treat him properly, but have as little to say to him as you can. I have been told that he spends much of his time at the stable and tavern, where he hears much profane and vulgar talk. Boys ought not to visit such places. By and by he will be smoking and drinking as bad as any of them."

"He smokes now," said Nat; "and he told Charlie one day that a boy could never be a man till he could smoke a 'long nine'."

"I hope you will never be a man, then," said his mother. "When a boy gets to going to the tavern to smoke and swear, he is almost sure to drink, and become a ruined man."

"I never do smoke, mother. I never go to the stable nor tavern, I don't associate with Sam and Ben Drake, nor with James Cole, nor with Oliver

Fowle, more than I can help. For I know they are bad boys. I see that the worst scholars at school are those who are said to disobey their parents, and every one of them are poor scholars, and they use profane language."

"That is very true, Nat," said his mother. "I am glad you take notice of these things. Bad boys make bad men; always remember that. Be very careful about the company you keep, for the Bible says, 'evil communications corrupt good manners.' You know how to behave well, and if you do as well as you can, you will be respected by all who know you."

"But, mother," asked Nat, "may I go over to Frank's house, and help him bury Trip? I won't be gone long."

"Yes, you may go, but it will be tea-time in an hour, and you must be back then."

Out ran Nat in a hurry, for he had stayed longer to converse with his mother than he meant to have done, and he was afraid Frank would get tired of waiting. He left Frank at the corner of the street, to wait until he ran home to ask his mother's permission to go with him to bury the dog. Now, many boys would have gone without taking this trouble. They would have taken the permission to go to Prospect Hill, to cover going to Frank's house also. But Nat would not do this. It would be taking advantage of his mother's kindness. He was never in the habit of going away even to the nearest neighbor's without permission. Such boys as Sam Drake are all over the neighborhood, and sometimes go even further, without consulting their parents. Very often their parents do not know where they are. If one of their associates should run home for permission to do a given thing, as Nat did, such a fellow as Sam Drake would be likely to say,

"I should like to see myself asking the old woman (his mother) to go there. If I wanted to go, I should go. What does a woman know about boys? I wouldn't be a baby all my days. If a fellow can't have his own way, I wouldn't give a snap to live. Permission or no permission, I would have the old folks know that I shall be my own man sometimes."

This is not manly independence, but youthful disobedience and recklessness, that lead to ruin. All good people look with manifest displeasure upon such an ungovernable spirit, and expect such boys will find an early home in a prison.

When Nat reached the corner of the street, he found that Frank had gone, so he hastened on, and was soon at Mr. Martin's (Frank's father).

"I waited a few minutes," said Frank, as he met Nat at the door, "and then I thought I would run on and get all things ready."

"I was afraid that I had kept you waiting so long that you got out of patience," added Nat. "But I stopped to tell mother about it, and she had considerable to say."

Frank had related the circumstances of Trip's death to his mother before Nat's arrival, and received her consent to bury the dog at the foot of the garden.

"Come, now, let us run into the wood-shed for a box," said Frank; "I have one there full of blocks that is just about right to put Trip into."

"Then you mean he shall have a coffin? I thought you would tumble him into his grave as they do dead soldiers on battle-fields."

"Not I. I have more respect for a *good* dead dog than that. Look here, is not that a capital box for it?" So saying he took up a small box full of blocks, that had once served him for play-things, and having taken the blocks out, he proceeded to lay Trip therein. His body just filled the box, as if it were made on purpose; and having nailed on the lid, they proceeded with it to the foot of the garden. They were not long in digging a grave, and soon the remains of Trip were decently interred. As the last shovel-full of dirt was thrown on, Nat gave utterance to a part of a declamation which he had spoken in school two weeks before. The portion he repeated was as follows:

"Not a drum was heard, nor a funeral note,
    As his corse to the ramparts we hurried;
Not a soldier discharged his farewell shot,
    O'er the grave where our hero we buried.

"Slowly and sadly we laid him down,
    From the field of his fame fresh and gory,
We carved not a line, we raised not a stone,
    But left him alone with his glory."

Frank smiled for the first time since Trip was kicked down the precipice, and said,

"Nat, you are always getting off your oratory; and I really think the occasion deserves a burst of eloquence. Poor Trip will never play hy-spy again; our good times with him are over."

"There, now I must hurry home to supper," said Nat, "mother will be waiting; so good-night till Monday."

Away he bounded homeward, and was just in season for his supper. After a thorough washing of face and hands, he sat down to the table with as keen an appetite as he ever had, his afternoon excursion having given him a good relish for food. The conversation naturally turned upon the fate of Trip, and the whole account of the tragedy was gone over again, with such comments thereon as each one was disposed to make.

"I have a very difficult lesson in arithmetic to dig out to-night for Monday," said Nat, as he rose from the table.

"Perhaps you will not be called upon to recite the lesson," replied his mother.

"Any scholar who gets rid of reciting a lesson which this teacher gives him must be one of the favorites," said Nat, not being the least suspicious that his mother was going to communicate any thing unpleasant. "For one, I want to recite it, after I have mastered it, and I know that I *can* master it. At any rate, I shall not give up beat until I have tried."

"Then you mean to belong to the 'try company' a while longer?" interrupted his mother.

"Yes, mother; the teacher read us some capital verses the other day on 'I'll try,' and she told a number of stories to illustrate what had been accomplished by trying."

"Your purpose is very good indeed, Nat, and I am sorry that we are not able to give you better advantages. But did you know that your services are in great demand? The agent of the factory has been after you this afternoon."

"For what?" asked Nat, with great surprise.

"To work in the factory to be sure. He wants a 'bobbin boy' very much, and thinks that you will make a good one; what do you say to it?"

"You didn't tell him that I would go, did you?"

"Well, your father and I have talked the matter over, and concluded that it will be necessary for you to do something for a living. We are poor, and your father does not see how he can support the family and keep you in school. The agent will give you two dollars a week, and this will be a great help to us."

"You can't mean, mother, that I am not to go to school any more?" inquired Nat.

"We do not know what may yet transpire in your favor, but for the present, at least, your schooling must cease."

Nat was almost overcome at this announcement, and his lips fairly quivered. His mother felt as badly as he did, though she exerted herself to conceal her emotion. At length she went on to say,

"I do not expect you will accede to this plan without a struggle with your love of study, but if it is best for us all that you should leave school and work in a factory, you can do it cheerfully, can you not?"

"I can do it," answered Nat, "but not cheerfully."

"I did not mean exactly that, when I spoke; for I expect you will do it only because our necessities make that change best."

"When does the agent want I should begin?" inquired Nat.

"On Monday. It is very short notice, but you may as well begin then as any time. There is one thing to be thought of for your advantage. You love to read, and the manufacturing company have a good library for the operatives. You can take out books, and read evenings."

"There will be scarcely any time for me to read after coming out of the factory at seven o'clock; and besides, after working from five o'clock in the morning until seven at night, I think I shall like the bed better than books."

"You will find as much time to acquire knowledge as ever Dr. Franklin did, and many other men who have been distinguished; and that is some encouragement."

"Last winter our teacher told Frank and I about Patrick Henry and Dr. Franklin, and he said that boys now have far better advantages. Do you suppose that the life of Dr. Franklin or the life of Patrick Henry will be in the library at the factory?"

"I have no doubt that both of them are there, and you can take the first opportunity to draw one of them out."

This last suggestion was a very important one to Nat. The prospect of having access to a good library made Nat almost willing to go into the factory. At any rate, after thinking the matter over, and becoming convinced that it was best for the family, as his mother said, that he should become a bobbin boy, and weighing the advantage of having a library to visit, he was quite reconciled to the arrangement. He was the eldest of the children, a large family, and it seemed reasonable that he should be required to do something for a livelihood, if necessity demanded. He knew very well that his parents would not have made such an arrangement, unless their low circumstances had forced them to it. Both of them highly valued a good school, and were interested in the education of their children, but their desires could not be gratified.

Saturday evening wore away, and the family dispersed for nightly repose. The last thoughts of Nat, ere he resigned himself to the arms of Morpheus, were of school and bobbins.

CHAPTER X.

THE NEW CALL.

Monday morning came to Nat, seemingly, before Sunday had time to get by. Thirty-six hours scarcely ever passed away so rapidly to him before. But it found him ready. He was one of the few boys who are always on hand, whether it was for school, or any thing else. Teachers never complained of him for being tardy, for they never had occasion to do it; and he was as prompt to recite his lessons as he was to be in school at nine o'clock. He was punctual to a second. If his mother told him to be at home at a given time from an afternoon visit or ramble, he was sure to be on the mark. He performed errands on the same principle, and never had to be called twice in the morning. The fact is, there was not a lazy bone in his whole body; each finger, toe, joint, and muscle, seemed to understand that it was made for action, and that it must hold itself in readiness to obey orders. His will, too, was king of his faculties, and not one of them would have presumed to disobey its ruler. The first little finger that would have dared to say *"no"* to his mandates, would have fared severely for its presumption.

Now, such a boy would not find it so difficult to rise early in the morning, at a precise time, to work in a factory, as a lazy one would. A lazy boy, who had been accustomed to get up when he pleased, and consequently was seldom ready to breakfast with the rest of the family, would have a hard time in breaking into such a factory life. The bodies of these indolent fellows seldom wake up all at once. After their eyes are fairly awake by much rubbing, opening, and shutting, their limbs have to be coaxed and persuaded to start. Now they think they will start up in just one minute, but the lazy body refuses, and one minute passes, and then another, until, sometimes, a whole hour is lost in the futile attempts of a weak will to make the limbs mind and get up. But Nat's will was law to his members.

He had been accustomed to hear the factory bell of his native village call others, but it never called him before. For this reason, he had never thought much about its tones, nor hardly stopped to consider that its call was very early. But now its very sound was different. It seemed to understand that Nat was to be called, and it did not require a very flighty imagination in him to perceive that it said Nat, as plainly as any bell could. He was on his feet in a moment. He did not wait for the bell to call twice, any more than he did for his parents to call twice. Every part of him waked up at once, from his head to his feet. His feet were as wide awake as his eyes, as any person would have inferred who had seen them start from the bed. If the bell had no harder case to arouse, it might have done its work with half the noise, and thus saved a great quantity of sound for special occasions, such as the fourth of July.

He was about the first to reach the factory on Monday morning.

"Hurrah! the bobbin boy is on hand," said the overseer as he entered.

"Yes, sir!" was Nat's short and modest reply.

"You'd rather go to school, I suppose," continued the overseer, "than to carry bobbins?"

"I had," answered Nat, "though I can do what is for the best."

"That's right. If everybody would do that, we should have a different world to live in."

The overseer said what he did to Nat, because he knew, as everybody else did in the village, that the boy loved his books. His brightness, and inclination to study, were themes of frequent remark among the people. In the school-room, his manner of acquitting himself attracted the attention of visitors. The teachers regarded him as a very promising boy, and often spoke of his talents. In this way, he was known generally in the community for his "intellectual turn." This explains the remark of the overseer about his loving school better than the factory.

One great surprise awaited Nat on that day. He found that Charlie Stone also became a factory operative on that morning. He did not know that Charlie expected to engage in this new business, nor did Charlie know that Nat did. Indeed, it was unexpected to both of them, since the agent made the arrangement with their fathers late on Saturday afternoon. The meeting of the two boys, therefore, in their new sphere of toil, was the occasion of mutual astonishment.

Charlie Stone was just the age of Nat—twelve years old—and was as good a boy as the neighborhood afforded. His father was poor, very poor indeed, and could not support his family by his own labor, so that Charlie was compelled to lend a helping hand, which he was willing to do. He was a very amiable boy, retiring and modest, a good scholar and associate. He was on intimate terms with Nat, so that their mothers used to say they were "great cronies." We have seen that they were in the same classes in school, and Charlie was really as good a scholar as Nat, though he had not the faculty of using his knowledge to so good advantage. He was a great reader, and he probably read much more than Nat in the course of a year. There is a great difference in boys, as well as men, about the ability to use the information acquired. One boy may thoroughly master his lessons, and fully understand the books he reads, and improve every moment of his time, and yet not be able to make his acquisitions tell so much as another of smaller attainments. His memory may not be retentive, and he may be kept back by a distrust of his own ability to do,—too bashful and timid to press forward. This was the case with Charlie. Nat, on the other hand, possessed a remarkable memory; together with a peculiar faculty to use his attainments to the best advantage. When he made an acquisition he knew how to use it. Every attainment seemed to run into wisdom and character, as the juices of the tree run into buds and fruit. Very small advantages appeared thereby to produce great results in his favor. Every one who knew him would agree, that what Richter said of himself was equally true of Nat, "I have made as much out of myself as could be made of the stuff, and no man should require more."

It was fortunate, on the whole, that these two boys entered the factory together, for both of them became more reconciled to their condition than they otherwise would have been. They were company for each other, and, if possible, became more strongly attached to each other in consequence. They had no opportunity, during the forenoon, to converse with each other concerning the manner of their having entered the factory. But as soon as the rattling machinery silenced its clatter for the dinner hour, the subject was talked over until both fairly understood it.

"Come," said Nat, as they passed out of the factory, "let us step into the office and see when we can take out books."

"Perhaps Dr. Holt (the agent) has gone to his dinner?"

"We'll see," added Nat. So saying they both walked into the office.

"What is wanted, boys?" inquired the doctor, who was there, and he smiled upon them so benignantly that they could not but feel at home.

"We stepped in, sir, to inquire when we could take books out of the library," answered Nat.

"To-night, my lads, as soon as the factory stops. So it seems you are going to improve your spare moments reading?"

"Yes, sir," replied both of them together.

"That is right. It is not the worst berth in the world to be a factory boy, especially if there is a good library to use. Two hours a day in reading will do a great deal for a boy. Most of the young people waste time enough to acquire an education, if it were only well improved. You will have more time for self-improvement than William Cobbett had in his youth—that distinguished member of the British Parliament, of whom so much has been said in the papers of late."

The doctor was an intelligent, well-read man, affable and kind, and deeply interested in the welfare of those over whom he had an oversight. The boys particularly shared his tender sympathies, especially such bright ones as the two who stood before him. His words were uttered in such a way as to go straight to the heart of an enterprising lad. They were words of cheer and hope, such as give spirit and pluck to a poor fellow whose experience is shadowy, to say the least. More than one boy has had occasion to remember the doctor with gratitude. His allusion to William Cobbett, really contained more information than he imparted, as the following account which Cobbett published of himself will show:—

"I learned grammar," said he, "when I was a private soldier on the pay of sixpence a day. The edge of my berth, or that of my guard-bed, was my seat to study in; my knapsack was my book-case; a bit of board lying on my lap was my writing table; and the task did not demand any thing like a year of my life. I had no money to purchase candle or oil; in winter time it was rarely that I could get any evening light but that of the fire, and only my turn of even that. And if I, under such circumstances, and without parent or friend to advise or encourage me, accomplished this undertaking, what excuse can there be for any youth, however poor, however pressed with business, or however circumstanced as to room or other conveniences? To buy a pen or a sheet of paper I was compelled to forego some portion of food, though in a state of half starvation; I had no moment of time that I could call my own; and I had to read and write amidst the talking, laughing, singing, whistling, and brawling of at least half a score of the most thoughtless of men, and that, too, in the hours of their freedom from all control. Think not lightly of the farthing that I had to give, now and then, for ink, pen, or paper! That farthing was, alas! a great sum to me! I was as tall as I am now; I had great health and great exercise. The whole of the money, not expended for us at market, was two- pence a week for each man. I remember, and well I may, that on one occasion I, after all necessary expenses, had, on Friday, made shifts to have a halfpenny in reserve, which I had destined for the purchase of a red herring in the morning; but when I pulled off my clothes at night, so hungry then as to be hardly able to endure life, I found that I had lost my halfpenny! I buried my head under the miserable sheet and rug, and cried like a child! And again I say, if I, under circumstances like these, could encounter and overcome this task, is there, can there be, in the whole world, a youth to find an excuse for the non-performance?"

Nat had no time to converse with his parents at noon concerning his new business—his time was occupied, after dinner, until the factory bell rung, in giving a history of his surprise at meeting Charlie there. His parents were surprised too, as they had not heard that he intended to work in the mill.

"I am glad for you," said his mother, "that Charlie is to work with you, though I am sorry that his parents are so poor as to make it necessary. Charlie is a noble boy, and I know you have a good companion when you have him."

"We can take books from the library to-night," said Nat.

"And what one are you going to take out?" inquired his mother.

"The Life of Patrick Henry," was his quick reply.

"What is there about Patrick Henry that interests you in his life?"

"He was a great orator and statesman, and made himself so by improving his time, so the teacher told us last winter."

Nat was obliged to hasten back to the factory at the call of the bell, so that a period was put to the conversation very suddenly. His work in the factory was to carry bobbins around to the operatives as fast as they wanted them, and hence he was called "The Bobbin Boy." It was rather light work though he was often obliged to step around quite lively, which he could do without much trouble, since he was none of your half-way boys. His movements were quick, and what he did he did with all his heart, with only occasional exceptions. A smart, wide-awake, active boy could carry bobbins to better advantage than a clumsy man in meridian life. Nat carried them as if he were made on purpose for the business. It was difficult to tell which he did best, carry bobbins or speak pieces. He did both, as a looker-on said, "in apple-pie order," which means, I suppose, about as well as they could be done by one of his age.

At the close of the day, when the boys came to take out books, Nat found that the life of Patrick Henry was out, so he took the life of Dr. Franklin, without feeling much disappointed. He was so anxious to read both of these volumes that he cared but little which he read first.

"That you, Nat?" exclaimed David Sears, with whom Nat met on his way home from the factory. "What's got you to-day? We missed you and Charlie at school."

"Done going to school," answered Nat. "We are going to finish our education in the factory."

"You have graduated in a hurry, it seems to me. But you don't mean that you are not going to school any more, do you?"

"Why, yes; I think that will really be the case, though I hope for the best," replied Nat. "Perhaps I may go again after a while."

"It is really too bad," continued David. "I wish the factory was a thousand miles off. It is a pretty hard case to be tied up to a factory bell every day, and work from five o'clock in the morning till seven at night."

"I don't care much about the bell," replied Nat. "I can get up as early as the man who rings it, I know. And then it is capital to make one punctual. There is no chance for delays when the bell calls—a fellow must be on the mark."

Nat struck upon a very important thought here. Punctuality is a cardinal virtue, and the earlier a person learns to be punctual the better it is for him. Being obliged to obey the summons of a bell at just such a minute aids in establishing the habit of punctuality. Hence, the modern rules of the school- room, requiring pupils to be there at a precise hour, and to recite their lessons at such a minute, are very valuable to the young. Pupils who form the habit of getting to school any time in the morning, though usually late, are generally behind time all the way through life. They make the men and women who are late at meeting, late to meet their business engagements, late everywhere—a tardy, dilatory, inefficient class of persons, wherever they are found. It is good to be obliged to plan and do by car-time. The man who is obliged to keep his watch by railroad time, and then make all things bend to the same, is more likely to form the habit of being punctual, than he who has not a fixed moment for going and coming. And so it is with the factory. The boy who must be up at the first bell-call, and get to his place of toil at five o'clock in the morning, is more likely to be prompt in every place and work. Nat was right. It is another instance of his ability to perceive the real tendencies of things.

David smiled at Nat's view of the matter, and asked, "What book have you there?"

"The life of Dr. Franklin. You know they have a library for the operatives in the factory, and I mean to make the most of it."

"But you won't get much time to read, if you work in the factory all day, from Monday morning till Saturday night."

"I can get two or three hours in a day, if I sit up till ten o'clock, and that is early enough for anybody to go to bed. I shall read this volume through by Saturday night."

"Well, *you'll* make the most of it if anybody can," said David, laughing, and hurrying on homewards.

Nat commenced reading Dr. Franklin's life that evening. It was his first step in a somewhat systematic course of reading, for which he was indebted to the manufacturing company. But for his factory life he might not have been introduced to those authors that gratified his desire for knowledge, and nurtured in his soul that energy and perseverance which he was already known to possess.

His parents did not converse much with him about his new business, as they thought it might not be wise; but they interested themselves in his reading. His mother found he was deeply absorbed in Franklin's life, though he said but little of the book, except in reply to her inquiries. But he seemed hardly willing to lay it aside at bed-time, and eagerly took it up to read during the few spare moments he had when he came to his meals. The book was read through before the next Sabbath.

CHAPTER XI.

THE LOFTY STUDY.

Some time after Nat donned the bobbin boy's suit, he proposed to Charlie to come over and spend his evenings with him for mutual improvement.

"I have a nice place to read and study all by myself," said he, "and I want to talk over some subjects we read about with you. Besides, what do you say to studying mathematics together a portion of the time? I think we can get along about as well in this branch as we could to have a teacher."

"*I* should like it first rate," answered Charlie. "Mathematics is your hobby, and I think I can make good improvement under your tuition."

"I don't propose to teach, sir," added Nat, "but to learn. I will get what I can out of you, and you may get what you can out of me. That is fair, I am sure. You will get what you can out of me just as cheap as I get what I can out of you. It will not be a very expensive school as you see."

"Agreed," said Charlie. "I will be at your house this evening by the time you are ready for me."

Charlie was true to his engagement, and by the time Nat was ready to ascend to his study, a rap announced his arrival. With lamp in hand, Nat led the way up two flights of stairs, and introduced Charlie into the attic, saying,

"This is my study. I have permission to use this for a sanctum as long as I please."

"It is a lofty one, surely," responded Charlie. "You can't get up much higher in the world if you try."

"When we get into astronomy, all we shall have to do will be to bore a hole through the roof to make our observations. Could any thing be more convenient?"

The reader need not smile at Nat's study. It was better than the first one that the renowned Dr. John Kitto had. Like Nat's, Kitto's first study was in his father's attic, which was only seven feet long and four feet wide. Here a two-legged table, made by his grandfather forty years before, an old chest in which he kept his clothes and stationery, and a chair that was a very good match for the table, together with what would be called a bed by a person who had nothing better, constituted the furniture. Also, the time-honored St. Pierre was worse off even when he wrote his celebrated "Studies of Nature." His study was a garret, less capacious than that which Nat occupied, and there he spent four years of his life in the most laborious study.

Night after night Nat and Charlie met in the aforesaid attic, to read, study mathematics, and discuss the subjects of the volumes which they read. They made very commendable progress in mathematics, and probably kept in advance of their companions who were in school. Among the characters who were discussed by them, none received more attention than Dr. Franklin and Patrick Henry.

"Which of these characters do you like best?" inquired Charlie one evening.

"I suppose that Dr. Franklin would be considered the best model; but such eloquence as that of Patrick Henry must have been grand. Dr. Franklin was not much of a speaker, though what he said was sound and good."

"And Patrick Henry was a lazy fellow when he was young," added Charlie. "You remember that his father set him up in business two or three times, and he failed because he was too shiftless to attend to it."

"Very true; and he suffered all through life on account of not having formed habits of industry, economy and application. It shows what a splendid man he might have made, if he had reduced Franklin's rules to practice."

"Let us read over those rules of Franklin again," said Charlie. "You copied them, I believe."

Nat took up a paper, on which the rules were penned in a handsome hand, and proceeded to the following:

1. "TEMPERANCE.—Eat not to dulness; drink not to elevation.

2. SILENCE.—Speak not but what may benefit others or yourself; avoid trifling conversation.

3. ORDER.—Let all your things have their places; let each part of your business have its time.

4. RESOLUTION.—- Resolve to perform what you ought; perform without fail what you resolve.

5. FRUGALITY.—Make no expense but to do good to others or yourself; that is, waste nothing.

6. INDUSTRY.—Lose no time; be always employed in something useful; cut off all unnecessary actions.

7. SINCERITY.—Use no hurtful deceit; think innocently and justly; and, if you speak, speak accordingly.

8. Justice.—Wrong none by doing injuries, or omitting the benefits that are your duty.

9. Moderation.—Avoid extremes; forbear resenting injuries as much as you think they deserve.

10. Cleanliness.—Tolerate no uncleanliness in body, clothes, or habitation.

11. Tranquillity.—Be not disturbed at trifles, or at accidents common or unavoidable.

12. Humility.—Imitate Jesus and Socrates."

"There is scarcely one of those rules that Patrick Henry observed in his youth," said Charlie. "After he got to be a man grown, and his friends were all out of patience with him, and he was absolutely compelled to do something, or starve, then he began to apply himself."

"Yes; and what a commotion he made!" responded Nat. "That first plea of his against the clergy of Virginia on the tobacco Act, when he won the case against fearful odds, and the spectators were so excited by his oratory that they carried him out of the court room on their shoulders, is the best thing that I ever read of any orator. It was not his learning nor his argument, but his eloquence that gave this power over his hearers."

"And it was just the reverse with Dr. Franklin," said Charlie. "It was his wisdom, solid common sense, and worth of character, that enabled him to carry his points, and that I think is far more valuable."

"I learned one thing," said Nat, "from the life of Patrick Henry, which I never knew before, that he owed his final success more to his close observation of men and things than to the study of books. He learned something from every thing he saw and heard. Eye-gate and ear-gate were always open. He observed his companions closely when he was young, and told stories to witness the different feelings they would awaken in the hearts of different associates. In fact, he did not learn near so much from books as he did from men. And afterwards, when he had law students to instruct, one of his lessons was, 'study men and not books.'"

"Well, Nat, you are something like him," said Charlie, smiling. "You are always seeing some thing to learn, where I should never think of looking."

"Precious little like him," responded Nat, "but I intend to profit in future by what I learned from Patrick Henry's life."

"I mean just as I say, Nat, truly, you are like him now, a little. Last summer you was determined to know why the water was warmer in windy weather than it was in a calm; and I believe you found out before we went in a swimming the next time. And as for studying men, you are always up to that. I don't believe there is an operative in the factory whose qualities you have not settled in your own mind. You learned more of that fellow they turned away, by looking at him, than others found out by talking with him."

It was true that Nat was thus accustomed to observe and inquire into the *whys* and *wherefores* of things. For this reason he was never satisfied with a lesson until he understood it, unless we except the study of grammar. He formed his opinions of all his associates, and knew one to be selfish, another to be ill-tempered, another generous, and so on. He was probably attracted by Patrick Henry's study of men, on account of this disposition in himself, although he was not altogether conscious of it. But this quality enabled him to learn much that otherwise he would not have known. For when he was not reading a book, men, women, and children were around him, and many events were transpiring, all of which he could study. Thus he found teachers everywhere, and books everywhere, not indeed such books as are used in schools or fill the shelves of libraries, but such as are furnished in the shape of incidents, and such as are bound up in flesh and bones. He could read the latter while he was carrying bobbins in the factory, and walking the streets, or going to meeting. In this way he would be learning, learning, learning, when other boys were making no progress at all.

Shakspeare, the world's great dramatist, must have been indebted to this faculty of observation, far more than to books and human teachers, for his inimitable power of delineating human nature. He was the son of a poor man, who could not read nor write, according to reports, and he went to London to live, where he held horses for gentlemen who visited the theatre, receiving small remuneration for his labor. From holding horses outside, he came to be a waiter upon the actors within, where he must have been a very close observer of what was said and done; for his brilliant career began from that hour, and he went on from step to step until he produced the most masterly dramatic works, such as the world will not let die. There is no doubt that he was a born poet, but it was his faculty to read men and things that at last waked the dormant powers of the poet into life. He saw, investigated, understood, mastered, and finally applied every particle of information acquired to the work that won him immortal fame.

"Nat, you are the best penman in the mill," said Dr. Holt to him one day, as his attention was called to a specimen of his handwriting. "Where did you learn to write so well?"

"At school, sir," was his laconic reply.

"But how is it that you learn to write so much better at school than the other boys?"

"I don't know, sir!" and he never said a more truthful thing than he did in this reply. For really he did not know how it was. He did not try very hard to be a good penman. He did many other things well, which did not cost him very much effort. It was easy for him to get the "knack" of holding his pen and cutting letters. He would do it with an ease and grace that we can only describe by saying it was Nat-like. It is another instance, also, of the advantage of that principle or habit, which he early cultivated, of *doing things well*. As one of his companions said,

"He can turn his hand to any thing."

One evening in October, when the harvest moon was emphatically "the empress of the night," and lads and lasses thought it was just the season for mirth and frolic, the boys received an invitation to a party on the following evening.

"Shall you go?" inquired Charlie, when they were in the attic study.

"I should like to go, but I hardly think I shall. I want to finish this book, and I can read half of it in the time I should spend at the party."

"As little time as we get to study," added Charlie, "is worth all we can make of it; and Dr. Franklin says in those rules, 'lose no time.' I shall not go."

"I don't think that all time spent in such a social way can be called 'lost,' for it is good for a person to go to such places sometimes. But I think I shall decide with you *not to go*. I suppose that some of the fellows will turn up their noses, and call us 'literary gentlemen,' as Oliver did the other day."

"Yes; and Sam said to me yesterday as I met him when I was going home to dinner, 'fore I'd work in the factory, Charlie, and never know any thing. You look as if you come out of a cotton-bale. I'll bet if your father should plant you, you'd come up cotton,' and a whole mess of lingo besides."

"And what did you say to him?" asked Nat.

"Not much of any thing. I just said, 'if I don't look quite as well as you do, I think I know how to behave as well,' and passed on."

That Nat met with a good many discouraging circumstances, must not be denied. It was trying to him occasionally to see other boys situated much more favorably, having enough and to spare; and now and then a fling, such as the foregoing, harrowed up his feelings somewhat. He was obliged to forego the pleasure of many social gatherings, also, in order to get time to study. Sometimes he went, and usually enjoyed himself well, but often, as in the case just cited, he denied himself an evening's pleasure for the sake of reading.

About this time, when he felt tried by his circumstances, he said to his mother,

"I don't know much, and I never shall."

"You haven't had an opportunity to know much yet," answered his mother. "If you continue to improve your time as you have done, I think you will be on a par with most of the boys."

"But poor boys have not so good a chance to stand well, even if they have the same advantages, as the sons of the rich."

"I am not so sure of that," replied his mother. "I know that money is thought too much of in these days, and that it sometimes gives a person high position when he does not deserve it. But, as a general thing, I think that character will be respected; and the poorest boy can have a good character. Was not that true of all the good men you have been reading about?"

Nat was obliged to confess that it was, and the conversation with his mother encouraged him, so that he went to his reading that evening, with as much pluck as ever. The more he learned, the more he wanted to know; and the faster he advanced, the higher he resolved to ascend.

CHAPTER XII.

THE DEDICATION.

Soon after Nat entered the factory, a hall was erected in the village, and dedicated to literary purposes. Nat was all the more interested in the event because it was built under the auspices of the manufacturing company for whom he worked, and their library was to be somehow connected with the institute that would meet there.

"No reading to-morrow night," said he to Charlie, as they closed their studies on the evening before the dedication. "We must go to the dedication of the hall without fail. I want to know what is to be done there."

"They say the library is going up there," answered Charlie. "Have you heard so?"

"Yes; but we shall have just the same privileges that we do now, and I expect the library will be increased more rapidly, because they are going to make provisions for others to take out books by paying, and the money goes to enlarge the library."

"But the more persons there are to take out books, the more difficult it will be to get such books as we want," said Charlie. "Do you not see it?

"Yes; but then 'beggars must not be choosers,' I suppose," Nat answered with a quizzical look. "*Your* chance will be poorer than mine in that respect, for you read more books than I do, and of course you will want more."

Nat was in season at the dedication, and secured a seat near the platform, where he could see and hear the speaker to the best advantage. He was not there, as doubtless some boys were, just to see what was going on; but he was there to *hear*. An address was to be delivered by a gentleman whose reputation would naturally create the expectation of an intellectual treat, and that address was what Nat wanted to hear. It was singular that the lecture should be upon the life and character of a self-made man, of the stamp of Dr. Franklin and others, whose biographies our young hearer had read with the deepest interest. But so it was. The subject of the address was Count Rumford; and you might know that Nat swallowed every word, from the leading points of it, which were in substance as follows:—

The real name of Count Rumford was Benjamin Thompson. He was born in Woburn, Mass., in the year 1752. His father was a farmer in humble circumstances, and he died when Benjamin was an infant. His mother was only able, when he attained a suitable age, to send him to the common school. He was a bright boy, though he was not so much inclined to study books. He preferred mechanical tools, with which he exhibited considerable ingenuity in constructing various articles, particularly rough drafts of machinery. Among other things he sought to produce a model of perpetual motion. He was sure he could do it, and he set to work with a resolution worthy of a nobler enterprise. When one attempt failed, he tried again, and yet again, until his friends and neighbors called him a "simpleton," and openly rebuked him for his folly. His mother began to think he never would learn any craft by which he could gain a livelihood, and she was really discouraged. He was not vicious nor indolent. He had energy and perseverance, intelligence and tact; and still he was not inclined to choose any of "the thrifty occupations of human industry." At thirteen years of age he was apprenticed Mr. Appleton, a merchant of Salem, where he distinguished himself only by neatly cutting his name, "Benjamin Thompson," on the frame of a shop slate. He cared less for his new business than he did for the tools of the workshop and musical instruments, for which he had a decided taste. He soon returned to Woburn.

When he was about seventeen years of age, he began to think more seriously of studying, though most youth in poverty would have said, it is useless to try. But he had great self-reliance, and now he began to think that he could do what had been done by others. It would cost him nothing to attend the lectures on Natural Philosophy at Cambridge college, so he resolved to walk over there, a distance of nine miles, a step which laid the foundation of his future fame. In all weathers he persevered in attending the lectures, and was always punctual to a minute.

Soon after, he commenced teaching school in Bradford, Mass., and subsequently in Concord, N. H. In the latter place he became acquainted with the rich widow of Col. Rolfe, and, though only nineteen years of age, married her. But this calamity he survived, and acted a conspicuous part in the American Revolution. Soon after the battle of Bunker Hill, having lost his wife, he embarked for England, bearing despatches to the English government. There he soon became distinguished as a learned man and philosopher, and was elected a member of the Royal Society. He was knighted in 1784.

The King of Bavaria became acquainted with him, and, attracted by his marked abilities, appointed him to a high office of trust and responsibility in his court. There he reformed the army and established a system of common schools. He was strictly economical, and saved thousands of dollars to the Bavarian government, by "appropriating the paper used to teach writing in the military schools, to the manufacturing of cartridges by the soldiery."

He was a man of great kindness and benevolence, by which he was prompted to establish a reformatory institution for the mendicants of Bavaria, and so great was its success that it became renowned all over Europe. The sovereign conferred one honor after another upon him, and finally "created him a count by the name of Rumford, in honor of Concord, New Hampshire, whose original name was Rumford."

His writings upon philosophical subjects were valued highly, and widely circulated. He was a leader in founding the Royal Society of Great Britain. He gave five thousand dollars to the Academy of Arts and Sciences of Massachusetts to establish a premium to encourage improvement and discoveries, and a like sum to the Royal Society of Great Britain. He died in 1814, at the age of sixty-two, and by his will "bequeathed $1,000 annually and the reversion of his estate, to found the Rumford Professorship of Cambridge College, Mass.," to which University he felt much indebted for his early instruction in Natural Philosophy.

His life illustrates not only what a poor boy may become, but also what simple things a great man can do to promote the welfare of his fellow men. The military classes of Bavaria, and indeed all the poor of Europe, suffered for the want of food, and Count Rumford brought to their notice two articles of food to which they were strangers, healthful, nutritious, and cheap. The first was the use of the potato, which was raised only to a limited extent; but, through his exertions it came to be generally cultivated, much to the improvement of the condition of the poor. He received the gratitude of thousands for his efforts. The other blessing was the use of Indian corn in making *hasty-pudding*, which is a live Yankee invention. His instructions on this point shall be given in his own words, as they appeared in his essay written for European readers.

"In regard to the most advantageous mode of using Indian corn, as food, I would strongly recommend a dish made of it, that is in the highest estimation throughout America, and which is really very good and nourishing. This is called *hasty-pudding*, and is made in the following manner: A quantity of water, proportioned to the quantity of pudding to be made, is put over the fire, in an open iron pot or kettle, and a proper quantity of salt, for seasoning; the salt being previously dissolved in the water, Indian meal is stirred into it, little by little, with a wooden spoon with a long handle, while the water goes on to be heated and made to boil, great care being taken to put in the meal in very small quantities, and by sifting it slowly through the fingers of the left hand, and stirring the water about briskly at the same time with the spoon in the right hand, to mix the meal with the water in such a manner as to prevent lumps being formed. The meal should be added so slowly that when the water is brought to boil, the mass should not be thicker than water-gruel, and half an hour more at least, should be employed to add the additional quantity of meal necessary for bringing the pudding to be of the proper consistency, during which time it should be stirred about continually, and kept constantly boiling. The method of determining when the pudding has acquired a proper consistency, is this: the wooden spoon used for stirring it being placed upright in the kettle, if it falls down, more meal must be added; but if the pudding is sufficiently thick and adhesive to support the spoon in a vertical position, it is declared to be *proof,* and no more meal is added."

Then he goes on to teach them how to eat it. "The manner in which hasty-pudding is eaten, with butter and sugar or molasses, in America, is as follows: the hasty-pudding being spread out equally on a plate, while hot, an excavation is made in the middle with a spoon, into which excavation a piece of butter as large as a nutmeg is put, and upon it a spoonful of brown sugar, or, more commonly, molasses. The butter being soon melted by the heat of the pudding, mixes with the sugar or molasses, and forms a sauce, which being confined in the excavation made for it, occupies the middle of the plate. The pudding is then eaten with a spoon; each spoonful of it being dipped into the sauce before it is conveyed to the mouth; care being taken in eating it to begin on the outside, or near the brim of the plate, and to approach the centre by regular advances, in order not to demolish too soon the excavation which forms the reservoir for the sauce."

A great man must be very benevolent and humble to condescend to instruct the poor classes in raising potatoes and making hasty-pudding. The fact magnifies the worth of the man.

"Well, Nat, how did you like the address?" inquired his mother, after they reached home.

"Very much indeed," answered Nat. "I had no idea that the address was to be about Count Rumford. He makes me think of Dr. Franklin."

"You see that it is not necessary for a boy to have a rich father to buy him an education," continued his mother. "Where there is a will there is a way."

"I couldn't help laughing," said Nat, "to think of that great man teaching the people how to make hasty-pudding. I declare, I mean to draw a picture of him stirring a kettle of pudding."

His mother was quite amused at this remark and responded,

"I think the lecturer was right, when he said that such a condescending act by one so high in honor as Count Rumford, was a proof of his greatness. You remember that he said, 'a truly great man will do any thing necessary to promote the interests of his fellow-men.'"

Much more was said about the address, which we have not time to rehearse, and on the following morning, as Nat met Charlie at the factory, the latter remarked,

"What a fine lecture that was last night!"

"Yes," Nat replied; "it was just what I wanted to hear. My case is not quite hopeless after all. I think I could make a good professor of hasty-pudding."

Charlie laughed outright, and added, "I think I could learn to navigate that ocean of butter and molasses that he got up on the plate. A man ought to understand geometry and navigation to make and eat hasty-pudding according to his rule."

"I suppose," said Nat, after he had shaken his sides sufficiently over Charlie's last remark, "that he was applying Dr. Franklin's rule on 'FRUGALITY'—'make no expense but to do good to others or yourself.' That is it, I believe."

The mill started, and the conversation broke like a pipe-stem; but the lecture upon Count Rumford made a life-long impression upon Nat. It was exactly to his taste, and greatly encouraged him in his early efforts to acquire knowledge. It was much in his thoughts, and perhaps it had somewhat to do with his plans, some years after, when he himself walked to Cambridge to consult books in the library of the College, and to Boston to visit the Athenæum for the same object.

CHAPTER XIII.

A SCHOOL SCENE.

"They had quite a time at school yesterday," said Nat to Charlie, one morning during the winter following their entrance into the factory.

"What was it? I have heard nothing."

"The teacher had a real tussle with Sam Drake, and for a little while it was doubtful who would be master. They both fell flat on the floor, tipped over the chair, and frightened the girls badly."

"What did the teacher attempt to punish him for?"

"He wrote a letter to one of the boys about the teacher, and said some hard things, and the teacher got hold of the letter and read it. Then he called him up and made him spell before the school some of the words he had spelled wrong in the letter, at which they all laughed till Sam refused to spell any more. Then he doubled up his fist at the teacher, and defied him to whip him."

"He ought to have been flogged," said Charlie; "I hope he got his deserts."

"If reports are true, he did. Though it was a hard battle, the teacher made him beg at last, and they say the committee will turn him out of school to-day."

As the facts in the case were not quite as reports would have them, we shall give a correct history of the affair. Nat had heard an exaggerated report, and communicated it just as he received it. But the teacher did not have a hard time at all in conquering the rebellious boy, and neither of them fell on the floor. Neither did Sam shake his fist at him, and defy him to strike. The case was this:

The teacher observed a little commotion among the scholars, and inferred that some sort of game was being secretly played. On this account he tried to be Argus-eyed, and soon discovered a paper, as he thought, passed along from one scholar to another, that created considerable sensation. When it reached John Clyde, the teacher inquired:

"John! what have you there?"

After some hesitation, John answered "a paper," at the same time making an effort to conceal it.

"Be careful, sir," said the teacher; "*I* will take that document," and so saying, he stepped quickly to John's seat, and took the paper from his hand.

It proved to be a letter from Samuel Drake to Alpheus Coombs, and read as follows:

ALFEUS KOOMS,—if you will trade nives with me as we talked yisterday it will be a bargin for you, mine is jist as i telled you, or the world is flat as a pancake. Rite back and mind nothin about old speticles i don't care a red cent for his regilations about riting letters in school i shall do it when i please, and if he don't like it, he may lump it, he is a reglar old betty anyhow, and i kinder thinks his mother don't know he is out if he should happen along your way with his cugel, you may give him my complerments and tell him that I live out here in the corner and hopes he'll keep a respecterble distance, now rite back at once and show old speticles that the mail will go in this school-house anyhow. Your old Frend

SAMUEL DRAKE.

We have given the letter just as it was written, with its lack of punctuation, bad spelling and all. Samuel was accustomed to call the teacher "old speticles," because he wore glasses. The letter is a key to the character and attainments of a class of bad boys in every community, when they are about fifteen years of age.

The teacher took the letter to his desk, and carefully read it over, and then called out to its author, in a loud voice,

"Samuel! come into the floor."

Samuel knew that his letter was discovered then, and he hesitated.

"Samuel! come into the floor I say," exclaimed the teacher again, in a tone that was truly emphatic.

Samuel started, and took his place in the floor.

"Now turn round," said the teacher, "and face the school."

Samuel did as he was commanded, not knowing what was coming.

"Now spell Alpheus," said the teacher.

Some of the scholars who had read the letter began to laugh, as they now saw the design of the teacher. Samuel had his eyes open by this time, and saw what was coming. He hesitated and hung down his head.

"Be quick, sir. You shall have a chance now to exhibit your spelling acquisitions."

Samuel dared not refuse longer, so he began,

"A-l-al-f-e-fe-u-s-us."

"Pronounce it, sir."

"Alfeus."

The scholars laughed heartily, and the teacher joined them, and for three minutes the school-room fairly rung with shouts.

"Now spell Coombs," said the teacher.

"K-double o-m-s, kooms."

Again there was a roar of laughter in the room, which the teacher did not wish to suppress.

"Spell knife now; you are so brilliant that the scholars would like to hear more."

"N-i-f-e."

The scholars laughed again in good earnest, and the teacher added, "That is not the way to spell a very sharp knife."

"Spell bargain."

"B-a-r-bar-g-i-n-gin, bargin."

"Such a kind of a bargain, I suppose, as a poor scholar makes, when he wastes time enough in one winter to make him a good speller," continued the teacher. When the laughter had ceased, he put out another word.

"Spell spectacles."

"S-p-e-t-spet-i-speti-c-l-e-s-cles, speticles."

Some of the scholars really shouted at this new style of orthography.

"I suppose that is the kind of glasses that 'old speticles' wears," said the teacher. "You do not appear to entertain a very good opinion of him. You may spell respectable."

"I shan't spell any more," answered Samuel in an insolent manner.

"Shan't spell any more! I command you to spell respectable."

"I shan't spell it," replied Samuel more defiantly.

In another instant the teacher seized him by the collar, and with one desperate effort sent him half across the school-room. He hit the chair in his progress and knocked it over, and the teacher hit his own foot against the corner of the platform on which the desk was raised, and stumbled, though he did not fall. From this, the report went abroad that there was a sort of mélee in school, and the teacher was flung upon the floor in the scuffle. By the time Samuel found himself on his back, the teacher stood over him with what the young rebel called a cugel (cudgel) in his letter, saying,

"Get upon your feet and spell respectable loud enough for every scholar to hear."

The boy saw it was no use to contend with such strength and determination, and he instantly obeyed, under great mortification.

"R-e-re-s-p-e-c-spec-respec-t-e-r-ter-respecter-b-l-e-ble, respecterble."

The matter had assumed so serious an aspect by this time that the scholars were quite sober, otherwise they would have laughed at this original way of spelling respectable.

"Hold out your hand now," said the teacher, and at once the hand was held out, and was severely ferruled.

"Now you can take your seat, and await the decision of the committee. I shall hand them your letter to-night, and they will decide whether to expel you from school or not."

Samuel went to his seat pretty thoroughly humbled, and the teacher embraced the opportunity to give the scholars some good advice. He was a good teacher, amiable, affectionate, and laborious, but firm and resolute. He was too strict to please such indolent boys as Samuel, who often tried him by his idleness and stupidity. His object in making him spell as he did was to mortify him by an exposure of his ignorance. His father had given him good opportunities to learn, but he had not improved them, so that he could spell scarcely better than scholars eight years old. Had he been a backward boy, who could make little progress, even with hard study, the teacher would not have subjected him to such mortification; but he was indolent, and his ignorance was solely the fruit of idleness. On the whole, it was about as good a lesson as he ever had, and was likely to be remembered a good while. The district generally sustained the teacher in his prompt efforts to subdue the vicious boy.

The committee considered the case on that evening, and decided that Samuel should be expelled from school. They were influenced to decide thus, in part, by his many instances of previous misconduct. He was habitually a troublesome scholar, and they concluded that the time had come to make an example of him. Their decision was communicated to him by the teacher on the following day, and he was accordingly expelled. When he went out, with his books under his arm, he turned round and made a very low bow, which, though he intended it as an indignity, really savored more of good manners than he was wont to show.

In the sequel, the reader will understand why this incident is narrated here, and, by the contrast with Nat's habits and course of life, will learn that the "boy is father of the man" that "idleness is the mother of vice," and that "industry is fortune's right hand, frugality her left."

━━━━━━━━━━━━━━━━━━

CHAPTER XIV.

TAKING SIDES.

"I have been reading the Federalist," said Charlie one evening, as he entered Nat's study, "and I am a pretty good Federalist." He looked very pleasant as he spoke, and Nat replied in a similar tone and spirit, without the least hesitation,

"I have been reading the life and writings of Jefferson, and I am a thorough Democrat."

"A Democrat!" exclaimed Charlie, with a hearty laugh at the same time. "Do you know what a Democrat is?"

"Perhaps I don't; but if anybody is not satisfied with such principles as Jefferson advocated, he is not easily suited."

"But Jefferson was not a Democrat. The Federalist calls him a Republican."

"I know that," replied Nat. "The Jefferson party were called Republicans in their day; but they are called Democrats now. I don't like the name so well, but still the name is nothing in reality,—the principles are what we should look at."

"You don't like company very well, I should judge," said Charlie; "I should want to belong to a party that could say *we*."

"What do you mean by that?" inquired Nat.

"Father said there wasn't but four democratic votes cast in town at the last election; that is what I mean. I should think you would be lonesome in such a party."

"If *I* had been old enough," continued Nat, "there would have been *five* votes cast. I don't care whether the party is great or small, if it is only right."

"I glory in your independence," replied Charlie, "but I am sorry you have so poor a cause to advocate."

"I guess you don't know what the cause is, after all. Have you read the life of Jefferson?"

"About as much as *you* have read the Federalist," replied Charlie. "We are probably about even on that score."

This interview occurred some time after Nat and Charlie entered the factory, perhaps a year and a half or two years. Charlie really thought he was in advance of his fellow-student on this subject. He did not know that Nat had been reading at all upon political topics. Being himself the greatest reader of the two, he knew that he read upon some subjects to which Nat had given no attention. He was very much surprised to hear him announce himself a Democrat, and particularly for the reason named. It was about thirty years ago, when the followers of Jefferson were first called Democrats. Many of them were unwilling to be called thus, and for this reason they were slow to adopt the title. It was a fact that only four persons cast votes in Nat's native town, at the aforesaid election as avowed *Democrats*. But the incident shows that the hero of our tale was an independent thinker, voluntarily investigating some subjects really beyond his years, with sufficient discrimination to weigh important principles. In other words, he was a student, though a bobbin boy, loving knowledge more than play, and determined to make the most of his very limited opportunities. It is an additional proof of what we have said before, that he studied just as he skated or swam under water,—with all his soul,—the only way to be eminently successful in the smallest or greatest work.

"Let us see," said Nat, taking up the life of Jefferson, "perhaps *you* will be a Democrat too, when you know what Jefferson taught. *He* wrote the Declaration of Independence."

"He did!" exclaimed Charlie, with some surprise. "That is good writing certainly. It was read at the last Fourth of July celebration."

"And we will read some of it again," said Nat, opening the volume, "and then you may bring your objections."

"'We hold these truths to be self-evident,—that all men are created equal; that they are endowed by their Creator with certain inalienable rights; that among these are life, liberty, and the pursuit of happiness. That to secure these rights, governments are instituted among men, deriving their just powers from the consent of the governed; that whenever any form of government becomes destructive of these ends, it is the right of the people to alter or abolish it, and to institute a new government, laying its foundation on such principles, and organizing its powers in such form, as to them shall seem most likely to effect their safety and happiness.'"

"Have you any objections to that?" inquired Nat, after it was read.

"No," answered Charlie, "and I have never heard of any one who has. It is pretty good doctrine for such poor fellows as we are certainly."

"You are a Democrat so far, then," said Nat; "you want to have as good a chance as anybody, and so do I. I am for equal rights, and Jefferson would have the poor man have the same rights as a governor or president."

"So would the Federalists," replied Charlie. "John Adams wanted this as much as Jefferson."

"You mean that he said he did," answered Nat. "Jefferson thought that Mr. Adams's principles would lead to a limited monarchy, instead of a republic, where each man would enjoy his rights."

"I should like to know how that could be?" inquired Charlie. "What I have read in the Federalist shows that he was as much in favor of the Declaration of Independence as any one."

"But he wanted the president and his cabinet to have very great power, somewhat like monarchs, and Jefferson wanted the *people* to have the power. That was the reason that Jefferson's party called themselves Republicans."

"Yes; but do the Democrats now carry out the Declaration of Independence? Don't they uphold slavery at the present day?"

"Jefferson did not uphold it in the least, and a good many of his friends did not. If his life and writings tell the truth, some of the Federalists *did* uphold it, and some of them had slaves. So you can't make much out of that."

"All I want to make out of it," replied Charlie, "is just this—that the Democrats now *do* sustain slavery, and how is this believing the Declaration of Independence, that '*all* men are created equal?'"

"I don't care for the Democrats now," responded Nat. "I know what Jefferson believed, and I want to believe as he did. I am such a Democrat as he was, and if he was a Republican, then I am."

"I suppose, then," added Charlie, with a sly look, "that you would like the Declaration of Independence a little better if it read, 'all men are created equal,' *except niggers*?"

"No, no; Jefferson believed it just as it was, and so do I. Whether men are white or black, rich or poor, high or low, they are equal; and that is what I like. He never defended slavery, I would have you know."

"I thought he did," added Charlie.

"I can show you that he did not," said Nat, taking up a volume from the table. "Now hear this;" and he proceeded to read the following, in which Jefferson is speaking of holding slaves:

"'What an incomprehensible machine is man! who can endure toil, famine, stripes, imprisonment, and death itself, in vindication of his own liberty, and the next moment be deaf to all those motives whose power supported him through the trial, and inflict on his fellow men a bondage, one hour of which is fraught with more misery than ages of that which he rose in rebellion to oppose. But we must wait with patience the workings of an overruling Providence, and hope that that is preparing the deliverance of these our suffering brethren. When the measure of their tears shall be full—when their tears shall have involved heaven itself in darkness—doubtless a God of justice will awaken to their distress, and by diffusing a light and liberality among their oppressors, or, at length by his exterminating thunder, manifest his attention to things of this world, and that they are not left to the guidance of blind fatality.'"

"That is strong against slavery, I declare," said Charlie. "I had always supposed that Jefferson was a defender of slavery."

"How plainly he says that there is more misery in 'one hour' of slavery, than there is in 'ages' of that which our fathers opposed in the Revolution," added Nat.

"And then he calls the slaves *'our suffering brethren,'* and not *'niggers,'*" said Charlie, with a genuine look of fun in his eye.

"I want to read you another passage still, you are beginning to be so good a Democrat," said Nat.

"Don't call *me* a Democrat," answered Charlie, "for I don't believe the Democrats generally carry out the principles of Jefferson."

"Republican, then," answered Nat quickly, "just what Jefferson called himself. You won't object to that, will you?"

"Read on," said Charlie, without answering the last inquiry.

Nat read as follows:

"'With what execration should the statesman be loaded, who, permitting one half the citizens thus to trample on the rights of the other, transforms those into despots, and these into enemies, destroys the morals of the one part, and the *amor patriæ* of the other. For if a slave can have a country in this world, it must be any other in preference to that in which he is born to live and labor for another, in which he must lock up the faculties of his nature, contribute as far as depends on his individual endeavors to the banishment of the human race, or entail his own miserable condition on the endless generations proceeding from him. With the morals of a people their industry also is destroyed. For in a warm climate no man will labor for himself who can make another labor for him. This is so true, that of the proprietors of slaves, a very small proportion indeed are ever seen to labor. And can the liberties of a nation be thought secure when we have removed their only firm basis, a conviction in the minds of the people that these liberties are the gift of God? That they are not to be violated but with his wrath? Indeed, *I tremble for my country when I remember that God is just*; that his justice cannot sleep forever; that considering numbers, nature, and natural means only, a revolution of the wheel of fortune, an exchange of situation is among possible events; that it may become probable by supernatural interference. The Almighty has no attribute that can take side with us in such a contest. But it is impossible to be temperate and pursue this subject.'"

"That is stronger yet!" exclaimed Charlie. "I tell you, Nat, there are no such Democrats now."

"Yes, there are; you see one sitting in this chair," replied Nat, "and I believe there are many such. A person must believe so if he believes the Declaration of Independence. Come, Charlie, you are as good a Democrat as I am, only you won't own it."

"I certainly think well of Jefferson's principles, so far as you have read them to me, but I am not quite ready to call myself a Democrat."

We can readily see that Nat's sympathies would lead him at once to embrace the views of Jefferson on reading his life and writings. We have seen enough of him in earlier scenes to know in what direction they would run. His pity for the poor and needy, the unfortunate and injured, even extending to abused dumb animals; his views and feelings respecting the different orders of society; and his naturally kind and generous heart, would prepare the way for his thus early taking sides in politics. The traits of character discoverable in the court scene, when he plead the case of the accused boys; his grief with Frank when he wept over dead Trip; his condemnation of Sam Drake in defence of Spot, and one or two other incidents, are also traceable in his interest in the character and principles of Jefferson. There seemed to him more *equality* in those doctrines, more regard for the rights of the people, more justice and humanity, than in any thing he had read. Indeed, he had read nothing strictly political before, except what came under his eye in the papers, and he was fully prepared to welcome such views.

Jefferson's life and writings certainly made a lasting impression upon Nat's mind. It was one of the works that contributed to his success. Like the lives of Patrick Henry and of Dr. Franklin, and the address upon the character of Count Rumford, it contained much that appealed directly to his early aspirations. It is said that when Guido stood gazing upon the inimitable works of Michael Angelo, he was first roused to behold the field of effort for which he was evidently made, and he exclaimed, "I, too, am a painter." So, it would seem, that direction was given to the natural powers of Nat, and his thirst for knowledge developed into invincible resolution and high purpose by this and kindred volumes. It is often the case, that the reading of a single volume determines the character for life, and starts off the young aspirant upon a career of undying fame. Thus Franklin tells us that when he was a boy, a volume fell into his hands, to which he was greatly indebted for his position in manhood. It was "Cotton Mather's Essays to do Good," an old copy that was much worn and torn. Some of the leaves were gone, "but the remainder," he said, "gave me such a turn of thinking as to have an influence on my conduct through life; for I have always set a greater value on the character of a doer of good than any other kind of reputation; and if I have been a useful citizen, the public owes all the advantage of it to the little book." Jeremy Bentham said that the current of his thoughts and studies was decided for life by a single sentence that he read near the close of a pamphlet in which he was interested. The sentence was, "The greatest good of the greatest number." There was a great charm in it to one of his "turn of mind," and it decided his life-purpose. The passion of Alfieri for knowledge was begotten by the reading of "Plutarch's Lives." Loyola, the founder of the sect of Jesuits, was wounded in the battle of Pampeluna, and while he was laid up with the wound, he read the "Lives of the Saints," which impressed him so deeply that he determined from that moment to found a new sect.

There is no end to such examples from the page of history. It may seem an unimportant matter for a boy to read the life of Jefferson, or Franklin, or any other person; but these facts show us that it may be no trivial thing, though its importance will be determined by the decision, discrimination, and purpose with which the book is read. Very small causes are sometimes followed by the greatest results. Less than a book often settles a person's destiny. A picture created that life of purity and usefulness which we find in Dr. Guthrie, the renowned English champion of the Ragged School enterprise. His case is so interesting, that we close this chapter by letting him speak for himself. He says,

"The interest I have been led to take in this cause is an example of how, in Providence, a man's destiny,—his course of life, like that of a river, may be determined and affected by very trivial circumstances. It is rather curious,—at least it is interesting to me to remember,—that it was by a *picture* I was first led to take an interest in ragged schools,—by a picture in an old, obscure, decaying burgh that stands on the shores of the Firth of Forth, the birth-place of Thomas Chalmers. I went to see this place many years ago, and, going into an inn for refreshment, I found the room covered with pictures of shepherdesses with their crooks, and sailors in holiday attire, not particularly interesting. But above the chimney-piece there stood a large print, more respectable than its neighbors, which represented a cobbler's room. The cobbler was there himself, spectacles on nose, an old shoe between his knees,

—the massive forehead and firm mouth, indicating great determination of character, and, beneath his bushy eyebrows, benevolence gleamed out on a number of poor ragged boys and girls, who stood at their lessons round the busy cobbler. My curiosity was awakened; and in the inscription I read how this man, John Pounds, a cobbler in Portsmouth, taking pity on the multitude of poor ragged children left by ministers and magistrates, and ladies and gentlemen, to go to ruin on the streets,—how, like a good shepherd, he gathered in these wretched outcasts,—how he had trained them to God and to the world,—and how, while earning his daily bread by the sweat of his brow, he had rescued from misery and saved to society not less than five hundred of these children. I felt ashamed of myself. I felt reproved for the little I had done. My feelings were touched. I was astonished at this man's achievement; and I well remember, in the enthusiasm of the moment, saying to my companion (and I have seen in my cooler and calmer moments no reason for unsaying the saying),—'That man is an honor to humanity, and deserves the tallest monument ever raised within the shores of Britain.' I took up that man's history, and I found it animated by the spirit of Him who had 'compassion on the multitude.' John Pounds was a clever man besides; and, like Paul, if he could not win a poor boy any other way, he won him by art. He would be seen chasing a ragged boy along the quays, and compelling him to come to school, not by the power of a policeman, but by the power of a hot potato. He knew the love an Irishman had for a potato; and John Pounds might be seen running holding under the boy's nose a potato, like an Irishman, very hot, and with a coat as ragged as himself. When the day comes when honor will be done to whom honor is due, I can fancy the crowd of those whose fame poets have sung, and to whose memory monuments have been raised, dividing like the wave, and passing the great, and the noble, and the mighty of the land, this poor, obscure old man stepping forward and receiving the especial notice of Him who said, 'Inasmuch as ye did it to one of the least of these, ye did it also to me.'"

CHAPTER XV.

THREE IMPORTANT EVENTS.

"Frank is coming into the factory to work," said Nat one day to Charlie.

"He is?" answered Charlie with some surprise, as he had not heard of it; "when is he coming?"

"Next week I expect, if the place is ready for him. I am glad he is coming, for he will be company for us."

"Are his parents so poor that he is obliged to work here for a living?"

"Yes; they are not able to keep him at school any longer, and they think he is old enough now to do something to support himself."

"It is a dreadful thing to be poor, isn't it, Nat?"

"It is bad enough, but not the worst thing in the world," answered Nat. "Dr. Franklin said it was worse to be *mean*."

"I shan't dispute with him on that point," replied Charlie, "for there is only one side to that question. But I was thinking how poor boys are obliged to work instead of going to school, and of the many hard things they are obliged to meet."

"I think of it often," added Nat, "but then I remember that almost all the men whose lives I have read, were poor boys, and this shows that poverty is not so bad as some other things. But I don't quite believe Dr. Franklin's remark about the ease of becoming rich."

"What was his remark?" inquired Charlie.

"'The way to wealth is as plain as the way to market,'" answered Nat; "and if that isn't plain enough, I should like to know how it could be made plainer."

"Well, I don't believe *that*," said Charlie. "If men could become rich as easily as they can go to market, there would be precious few poor people in the world. But is that really what he means?"

"Certainly; only *industry* and *frugality*, he says, must be practised in order to get it."

"That alters the case," answered Charlie, "but even then I can't quite believe it. Are all industrious and frugal people wealthy?"

"No," replied Nat; "and that is the reason I doubt the truth of Dr. Franklin's remark. Some of the most industrious and frugal people in the world are poor."

The conversation was broken off here, and we will take this opportunity to remark, that Frank Martin entered the factory, as had been arranged, and was most cordially welcomed by the boys. He had been less with Nat, since the latter became a bobbin boy, than before, but their friendship was not abated. We have seen that they were on very intimate terms before, and were much in each other's society. Frank's entrance into the factory was suited to strengthen that friendship. The fact that each of the boys was poor and obliged to work for a living, and that each, also, was a factory boy, was enough to cause their sympathies to run together. It is natural for the rich to seek the society of the rich, and for the poor to seek the society of the poor, because their sympathies blend together. Hence, we generally find in communities that the rich and poor are usually separated, in some measure, by social barriers. This is not as it should be by any means; and this distinction between the rich and poor often becomes obnoxious to every kind and generous sentiment of humanity. Still, to some extent, the very experience of the rich begets a fellow-feeling with the rich, and so of the poor. The same is true, also, of trials. The mother who has lost her babe can sympathize with another bereaved mother, as no other person can. The sorrowing widow enters into the bitter experience of another wife bereft of her husband, as no other weeper can. And so it is of other forms of human experience. Then, the occupations of individuals comes in to influence the sympathies. A farmer meets a stranger, and finds, after cultivating his acquaintance, that he is a farmer, and this fact alone increases his interest in the individual. A sailor falls into company with an old man of four-score years, and finds that he was once a sailor, and this item of news draws him towards the aged man at once. A lawyer or clergyman is introduced to a gentleman in a foreign land, and he learns that the stranger is a lawyer or clergyman, as the case may be, and this knowledge itself makes him glad to see him.

Now this principle had a place in the hearts of these three factory boys, and bound them together by very strong ties of friendship. No three boys in the village thought so much of each other, nor were so much in each other's society, as they. There is no doubt that their intimate acquaintance and intercourse had much to do in forming the character of each. It certainly opened the way for some experiences that helped make Nat what he became.

"How did you like Marcus Treat?" inquired Charlie, the evening after he introduced this new comer into Nat's study.

"Very much indeed," answered Nat. "He seems to be a capital fellow, and he is a good scholar I know from his appearance."

"He *is* a good scholar, for one of the boys told me so. He has been in school only two or three weeks, but that is long enough to tell whether a fellow is a dunce or not."

"Where did he come from?" asked Nat.

"From——, I understand; and he lives with his uncle here. His parents are poor, and his uncle has offered to take him into his family."

"He will have a good home. His uncle will do as well by him as he would by a son."

"That is true; but he is not able to do much for either, I should think. Is he not a poor man?"

"Perhaps so; he has to work for a living, but many men who are obliged to do this, can do much for their sons. I pity him to have to leave his home and go among strangers."

"He will not be a stranger long with us," said Charlie. "He seemed much pleased to get acquainted with us, and to know about our plan of study."

"I suppose the poor fellow is glad to get acquainted with anybody," said Nat, "here among strangers as he is. It is a dreadful thing to be poor, you said, the other day, and I guess he begins to find it so. We must try to make him feel at home."

"That won't be difficult; for I think, from all I hear, that he fares much better here than he did at home, because his father was so very poor."

"They say 'home is home if it is ever so homely,' and I believe it, and probably Marcus does. But if he likes to study, he will be glad to join us, and we shall be glad to have him."

"I will speak to him about it to-morrow, if I see him," added Charlie. "He told me that he read evenings."

This Marcus Treat had just come to town for the reasons given by Charlie. He was about the age of Nat, and was a very bright, smart, active boy, disposed to do about as well as he knew how. He entered the public school immediately on coming into town, where his uncle designed to keep him, at least for a while. We shall find, hereafter, that he became a bosom companion of Nat's, and shared in his aspirations for knowledge, and did his part in reading, debating, declaiming, and other things pertaining to self-improvement.

A kind letter came that brought trial to Nat. It was designed for his good, but it dashed many of his hopes. An uncle, residing in a distant city, proposed to receive him into his family, and give him an opportunity to labor with himself in the factory. He was overseer of one of the rooms, and there Nat could work under his eye, in a new branch of the business.

"Would you like to go?" inquired his mother.

"On some accounts I should," answered Nat; "and on others I rather not go."

"It is a good thing for boys to go away from home to stay, if they can have a good place," said she; "and you would certainly enjoy being in your uncle's family."

"I should like that well enough; but it is going among strangers, after all; and then here I have a good chance to read and study, and Charlie and I have laid our plans for the future. We have but just commenced to do much in this respect. I should much rather stay here."

"But you can have books there, and as much time out of the factory as you have here. Your uncle will favor you all he can, and will be glad to see you try to improve your mind."

"I shan't have Charlie nor Frank there, nor that new acquaintance, Marcus, who was here the other evening; he was going to study with us. I don't believe there will be a library there either."

"I think there will be a library in the place," said his mother, "to which you can have access. At any rate, I am confident your uncle will provide a way for you to have all the books you want."

"How soon does he want I should come?"

"As soon as you can get ready. It will take me, some little time to repair your clothes, and make the new ones you must have. You could not be ready in less than two or three weeks."

"Perhaps I shall not like the new kind of work there, nor succeed so well in doing it. It will be more difficult."

"And you are able now to perform more difficult work than you did when you first went into the factory. You ought to keep advancing from one step to another. Besides, it may turn out better than you expect if you go there. You know that when you entered the factory two years ago, you thought you should never learn any thing more, but you have been pretty well satisfied with your opportunities to read. Perhaps you will be as happily disappointed if you go to live with your uncle."

"There is very little prospect of it," replied Nat. "But I shall do as you think best."

Nat could not help thinking about the new comer, Marcus Treat. He had been pitying him because he was obliged to leave his home, to live with his uncle among strangers; and now he himself was to have just such an experience. He little thought, when he was conversing with Charlie about this unpleasant feature of Marcus' life, that he would be obliged to try it himself so soon. But it was so. Marcus came to reside with his uncle in a community of strangers, and now Nat is going to reside with *his* uncle, where faces are no more familiar. It was a singular circumstance, and Nat could but view it in that light.

We have no space to devote to this part of Nat's life. We can only say, that it was decided to send him to his uncle's, and that he went at the earliest opportunity. It would be interesting to trace his interviews with his bosom companions before his departure—the sad disappointment that was felt by each party at the separation—the regrets of Charlie over frustrated plans in consequence of this step—the preparations for the journey—his leave of his native village—the long ride, by private conveyance, with his parents, to his new residence—and his introduction to a new sphere of labor.

He was absent three years, in which time he added several inches to his stature, and not a little to his stock of information. We will only say of this period, however, that his leisure hours were spent in self-improvement, and he was supplied with books, and had some other sources of information, such as public lectures, opened to him in the place. On the whole, these three years were important ones to him, so that there was a gain to set over against the loss he sustained in bidding adieu to well-laid plans for improvement in his birth-place.

CHAPTER XVI.

FINDING A LOST OPPORTUNITY.

It was a few weeks after Nat's return to his native place, where he was most cordially welcomed by his old companions, Charlie and Frank in particular. He was now an apprentice in the machine-shop, a stirring, healthy youth of about seventeen years.

"What have you there?" said Charlie to him, as he saw Nat take a book from his pocket to spend a leisure moment over it.

"My grammar," answered Nat, smiling.

"Have you discovered that you can't write a letter with propriety without it?" inquired Charlie, referring rather jocosely to a scene we have sketched.

"I am pretty thoroughly convinced of that," responded Nat. "At any rate, I shall find that lost opportunity if I can. Better now than never."

"You think better of that grammar class than you did five years ago, do you?"

"I have thought better of it for a good while, and should like to join it now if I had the opportunity. We were both very foolish then, as I have found out to my sorrow."

"I have often thought of that time," said Charlie; "I think we were rather too set in our opinions."

"Yes; and if the teacher had just given us what we deserved, perhaps I should not now be obliged to study grammar," added Nat.

"I am glad to see you so willing to own up, only it is a little too late to profit much by it. This 'after wit' is not the best kind."

"It is better than no wit at all," said Nat, rather amused at Charlie's way of "probing an old sore."

"The fact is, we were too young and green then to appreciate the teacher's reasons for wanting us to study grammar. He was right, and we were wrong, and now I am obliged to learn what I might have acquired then more readily."

"But we studied it, did we not?" inquired Charlie.

"Only to *recite*. We did not study it to *understand*. I knew little more about grammar when I left off going to school than I do about Greek or Hebrew. It is one thing to commit a lesson, and another to comprehend it. I am determined to understand it now."

"How long have you been studying it?"

"A few weeks ago I commenced it in earnest. I looked at it occasionally before."

"Have you advanced so far as to know whether Sam Drake is a proper or improper noun?" asked Charlie, in a jesting manner.

"Possibly," answered Nat, dryly. "By the way, I hear that Sam has removed from town, and all the family."

"Yes, they have gone, and I have cried none yet, and hope I shall not. Sam is a worse fellow now than he was when you left town."

"He is! He was bad enough then, and if he is much worse now, I pity the people who are obliged to have him about."

"They told some hard stories about him last summer; if half of them are true, he is a candidate for the state prison."

"What were the stories?" asked Nat, not having heard any thing in particular about him since his return.

"Some people thought he robbed Mr. Parton's orchard, and stole Mrs. Graves' pears and plums. He went off several times on Sunday and came back intoxicated. In fact, almost every evil thing that has been done in the night-time, for months past, has been laid to him. Perhaps he was not guilty, but people seem to think there is nothing too bad for him to do."

"And they think about right, too," added Nat. "I never saw a fellow who seemed to enjoy doing mischief like him. But how is it with Ben? I used to think he would do better if Sam would let him alone."

"People generally are of the same opinion. Ben is no worse than he was when he went to school, though he has frequently been in miserable scrapes with Sam. I guess they will end about alike. But I want to talk more about your grammar. Do you really expect to master grammar without a teacher?"

"Of course I do, or I should not undertake it. We conquered worse difficulties in mathematics than I have yet found in grammar."

"But how can you have patience to pursue such a dry study alone?"

"It is not dry now. It was dry to us that winter because we did not want to know any thing about it. Any book will be dry when we don't care to read it. I have found that no study is dry which I really want to know about. I like grammar first-rate now."

"Then you think that *we* were dry, and not the grammar?" inquired Charlie.

"Certainly; and you will find it so, if you will try it. When a person really wants to comprehend any subject, he will be interested in it, and he will quite readily master it."

"I shall not dispute your position," said Charlie. "But when you have a good grammar lesson you may recite it to me. I think you will make a good grammarian after all—you certainly will if a good resolution will accomplish it."

"I do not expect to distinguish myself in this branch of knowledge," replied Nat. "But I am determined to know something about it. A person need not learn every thing there is to be known about a study to make it profitable to him."

Nat was accustomed, at this period of his life, to carry some book with him for use every spare moment he found. He had a literary pocket into which volume after volume found its way, to remain until its contents were digested. The grammar had its turn in this convenient pocket, and every day was compelled to disclose some of its hidden knowledge. Pockets have been of great service to self-made men. A more useful invention was never known, and hundreds are now living who will have occasion to speak well of pockets till they die, because they were so handy to carry a book. Roger Sherman had one when he was a hard-working shoemaker in Stoughton, Mass. Into it he stuffed geography, history, biography, logic, mathematics, and theology, in turn, so that he actually carried more science than change. Napoleon had one, in which he carried the Iliad when he wrote to his mother, "With my sword by

my side, and Homer in my pocket, I hope to carve my way through the world."
Hugh Miller had one from which he often drew a profitable work as he was
sitting on a stone for a few moments' rest from his hard toils. Elihu Burritt had
one from the time he began to read in the old blacksmith shop until he acquired
a literary fame, and on "a grand scale set to working out his destiny at the
flaming forge of life." In writing to a friend, he said, "Those who have been
acquainted with my character from my youth up, will give me credit for
sincerity when I say, that it never entered into my head to blazon forth any
acquisition of my own. All that I have accomplished, or expect, or hope to
accomplish, has been, and will be, by that plodding, patient, persevering
process of accretion which builds the ant-heap,—particle by particle, thought
by thought, fact by fact. And if ever I was actuated by ambition, its highest and
warmest aspiration reached no further than the hope to set before the young
men of my country an example in employing those invaluable fragments of
time, called 'odd moments.'" He was once an agent for a manufacturing
company in Connecticut, and his pocket served him a noble purpose, for it
furnished him with a valuable work often, in unfrequented spots, where he
would let his horse rest, and spend a few moments in studying by the road-
side. The horse soon learned to appreciate the wants of his driver, and would
voluntarily stop in certain lonely retreats for him to pursue his studies. Thus
pockets that have carried the leanest purses, have often proved the greatest
blessing to mankind.

But how many youth there are, having much leisure time every day, who carry
nothing better than a knife, purse, and sometimes a piece of filthy tobacco, in
their pockets! It would be infinitely better for them to put a good book there,
to occupy their attention whenever a spare moment is offered. If only a single
hour in a day could be saved from absolute waste by such reliance on the
pocket, this would be sufficient to secure a large amount of information in a
series of years. The working-days of the week would yield, in this way, six
precious hours, equal to one day's schooling in a week, and fifty-two days, or
ten weeks of schooling in a year. Is not this worth saving? Multiply it by ten
years, and there you have one hundred weeks,—nearly two years of mental
culture. Multiply it by twenty, and you have about four years of this intellectual
discipline. Multiply it once more by fifty years (and he who lives to three score
years and ten, beginning thus in boyhood, will have even more time than that
for improvement), and you have nearly ten years of mental discipline. If we
could gather up all the wasted moments of the young, who prefer a jack-knife
to a book, what a series of years we could save for literary purposes! Nat's
pocket was worth a cart-load of those who never hold any thing more valuable
than money. If some kind friend had proposed to give him one well filled with
gold in exchange for his, he would have made a

poor bargain had he accepted the offer.

In regard to finding lost opportunities, few persons are ever so fortunate. Here and there one with the decision, and patient persevering spirit of Nat makes up for these early losses, in a measure, but they have to pay for it at a costly rate. Nat thought so when he struggled to master grammar without a teacher. Deeply he regretted that he let slip a golden opportunity of his early boyhood, when he might have acquired considerable knowledge of this science. But his perseverance in finally pursuing the study furnishes a good illustration of what may be done.

"What do you say to starting a debating society, Charlie?" inquired Nat, on the same day they discussed their grammar experience.

"I would like it well; and I think we could get quite a number to join it. Where could we meet?"

"We could probably get the use of the school-house, especially if a number of the scholars should join us. For such a purpose, I think there would be no objection to our having it."

"Let us attend to it at once," said Charlie. "Marcus and Frank will favor the movement, and I dare say we can get fifteen or twenty in a short time. Some will join it who do not think of debating, for the sake of having it go."

This reference to Marcus renders it necessary to say, that he had left the district school, and was learning the hatter's trade. During Nat's three years' absence, he was intimate with Frank and Charlie, and was disposed to improve his leisure time in reading. He was such a youth as would readily favor the organization of a debating society, and become an active member.

"Come over to our house early to-night," said Nat, "and we will see what we can do. If we form the society at all, we can do it within a week."

CHAPTER XVII.

THE PURCHASE.

On the same week, while the plans for a debating society were maturing, it was announced that the machine-shop would be closed on Saturday.

"I shall go to Boston then," said Nat.

"What for?" inquired Charlie.

"I want to look around among the bookstores; I think a few hours spent in this way will be of service to me."

"Going to purchase a library, I suppose?" added Charlie, with a peculiar twinkle proceeding from the corner of his eye.

"Not a very large one, I think; but it is well enough to see what there is in the world to make a library of."

"I should think it would be nothing but an aggravation to examine a bookstore and not be able to buy what you want. It is like seeing a good dinner without being permitted to eat."

"I can tell you better about that after I try it. After walking ten miles to enjoy the sight, and then returning by the same conveyance, I can speak from experience."

"Walk!" exclaimed Charlie; "do you intend to walk?"

"Certainly; won't *you* go with me? I should like some company, though it is not a very lonely way."

"I prefer to be excused," answered Charlie, "until I know your experience. But why do you not take the stage and save your shoe-leather?"

"Because shoe-leather is cheaper than stage-fare," replied Nat. "What little money I have to spare, I prefer to lay out in books. If the way to wealth was as plain as it is to Boston market,—as Dr. Franklin thought,—I should not only ride in the stage to the city, but also bring back a bookstore."

There was no railroad to the city at that time; but once or twice a day there was public conveyance by stage.

"Well, a pleasant walk to you," said Charlie; "I hope you will remember that you are nothing but a country boy when you meet our city cousins. I shall want to go some time, so you must behave well."

"Much obliged for your advice; I dare say it will be the means of saving me from everlasting disgrace. What do you charge for such fatherly counsel?"

"Halloo! here is Frank," exclaimed Charlie, as Frank made his appearance. "What do you think Nat is going to do on Saturday?"

"What he does every Saturday, I suppose,—work," answered Frank.

"No; there is no work to do on Saturday, and he is going to walk to Boston to visit the bookstores."

"Nobody can walk there quicker than Nat," replied Frank; "and if he scents a book, I shouldn't want to try to keep him company."

"I should think Boston was forty miles off by your talk," said Nat; "what is a walk of ten miles for any one of us, hale and hearty fellows. If I live, I expect to walk there more than once."

Saturday came. It was a bright, pleasant day, and Nat was up betimes, clothed and fed for a start. With a light heart and nimble feet, he made rapid progress on his way, and the forenoon was not far gone when he reached Cornhill. He was not long in finding the bookstores, caring, apparently, for little else. Most boys of his age, in going to the city, would be attracted by other sights and scenes. The Museum, with its fine collection of curiosities from every part of the world, would attract one; the State House, with its splendid view from the cupola, would draw another; the ships in the harbor, with their forest of masts, would fill the eyes of a third; while the toy-shops, music-stores, and confectioners, would command the particular attention of others. But none of these things attracted Nat. He went to examine the bookstores, and to them he repaired. Books filled the show-windows, and some were outside to attract attention. He examined those outside before he stepped in. He read the title of each volume upon the back, and some he took up and examined. Having looked to his heart's content outside, he stepped in. A cordial bow welcomed him to every place.

"What would you like, sir?" inquired one bookseller.

"I came in," replied Nat, "to look at your books, with yourpermission."

"Look as long as you please," replied the bookseller, with a countenance beaming with good-will, to make Nat feel at home.

For an hour or more he went from shelf to shelf, examining title-pages and the contents of volumes, reading a paragraph here and there, marking the names of authors, and all the while wishing that he possessed this, that, and the other work. There were two or three volumes he thought he might purchase if the price was within his limited means, among which was "Locke's Essay on the

Understanding." But he did not discover either of the works in his examination. At length he inquired,

"Have you a copy of 'Locke's Essay on the Understanding?'"

"Yes," replied the bookseller, "I have a second-hand copy that I will sell you cheap," taking down from a shelf an English pocket edition of the work. "There, I will sell you that for twenty-five cents."

"Is it a perfect copy?" inquired Nat, thinking that possibly some leaves might be gone, which would render it worthless to him.

"Yes, not a page is gone, and it is well bound, as you see."

"I will take it," said Nat, well pleased to possess the coveted volume so cheap, and especially that it was just the thing for his literary pocket. He was now more than paid for his walk to Boston. He had no idea of obtaining the work in a form so convenient for his use, and it was a very agreeable surprise.

In the course of the day, he made one or two other purchases, of which we shall not speak, and acquired many new ideas of books. Some valuable bits of knowledge he gleaned from the pages over which his eyes glanced, so that, on the whole, it was a day well spent for his intellectual progress.

It is related of Dr. John Kitto, that in his boyhood, when he first began to gratify his thirst for knowledge, he was wont to visit a bookseller's stall, where he was privileged to examine the volumes, and he there treasured up many a valuable thought, that contributed to his future progress and renown. He always regarded this small opportunity of improvement as one of the moulding events of his life.

Nat was on his way home at a seasonable hour, and had a very sociable time with his new pocket companion, which he could not help reading some on the road. It is doubtful if he ever spent a happier day than that, though he knew little more about Boston than he did in the morning, except about the extent and attractions of its bookstores, with a half dozen of which, on Cornhill and Washington street, he became familiar.

"Good morning, Nat," said Charlie, on Monday morning, as they met at the shop. "What discoveries did you make in Boston?"

The only reply that Nat made was to take from his pocket, and hold up "Locke's Essay on the Understanding."

"What is that?" inquired Charlie, taking the volume from Nat's hand, and turning to the title-page.

"I have been wanting that some time," said Nat, "but I had no idea of finding a pocket edition nor getting it so cheap. I bought that for twenty-five cents."

"It is a second-hand copy, I see."

"Yes; but just as good for my use as a copy fresh from the press."

"A good fit for your pocket," said Charlie; "I should think it was made on purpose for you. Has the grammar vacated it?"

"To be sure; it moved out the other day, and Locke has moved in," replied Nat, taking up Charlie's witticism.

"Did you have a good time in the city?"

"Capital: so good that I shall go again the first opportunity I have. But, I confess, it was rather aggravating to see so many books, and not be able to possess them."

Charlie smiled at this confession, remembering their conversation a few days before, and both proceeded to their work.

This new volume was a great acquisition to Nat, and as much as any other, perhaps, had an influence in developing and strengthening his mental powers. It was not read and cast aside. It was read and re-read, and studied for months, in connection with other volumes. It was one of the standard books that moulded his youth, and decided his career.

It is a singular fact that "Locke's Essay on the Understanding" has exerted a controlling influence upon the early lives of so many self-taught men. It was one of the few volumes that constituted the early literary treasure of Robert Burns, to which he ascribed much of his success, though he says, at the same time, "A collection of English songs was my *vade mecum*." The famed metaphysician, Samuel Drew, owed his triumphs mainly to this work. True, he became a great reader of other works, for he said, "The more I read, the more I felt my ignorance; and the more I felt my ignorance, the more invincible became my energy to surmount it. Every leisure moment was now employed in reading one thing or another. Having to support myself by manual labor, my time for reading was but little, and to overcome this disadvantage, my usual method was to place a book before me while at meat, and at every repast I read five or six pages." Yet, he attached the most importance to "Locke's Essay," for he acknowledged that it turned his attention to metaphysics, and, he said, "It awakened me from my stupor, and induced me to form a resolution to abandon the grovelling views which I had been accustomed to entertain."

The German scholar, Mendelsohn, owed not a little of his distinction in certain departments of study to the influence of a Latin copy of "Locke's Essay." He was an extensive reader, and found that a knowledge of Greek and

Latin was necessary for the successful prosecution of his literary pursuits. Consequently he purchased a copy of "Locke's Essay" in Latin, and with an old dictionary, which he bought for a trifle, and the assistance of a friend, who understood Latin, fifteen minutes each day, he translated the work. But the knowledge it gave him of Latin was far less valuable than the teachings it communicated, and which he incorporated into the very web of his future life.

We can readily perceive how a work like this is suited to arouse the dormant energies of the mind, and start it off upon a career of thought and influence. That knowledge of human nature which it imparts, and particularly the Philosophy of the Mind which it unfolds, are suited to aid the orator and statesman. He who understands these laws of human nature can more surely touch the springs of emotion in the soul, by the flow of his fervid eloquence.

This was not the last visit of Nat to the Boston bookstores. Subsequently, as he had opportunity, he walked to the city on a similar errand, and always returned with more knowledge than he possessed in the morning.

CHAPTER XVIII.

THE DEBATING SOCIETY.

The plans of Nat for a debating society were successful, and arrangements were made accordingly. Permission was obtained to use the school-house for the purpose, and Tuesday evening was appointed as the time to organize.

"Much will depend upon beginning well," said Nat to Marcus. "We must make it a good thing if we expect any favors in the village."

"Shall we admit spectators?" inquired Marcus.

"After we have fairly commenced," answered Nat. "There won't be much room, however, if all the members attend, and other young people who want to come in."

"I should think it would be well to have some declamations and dialogues occasionally," added Marcus; "it will give more variety. I imagine that our debates will want something else to back them up. And then some will be willing to declaim who will not attempt to debate."

"That is true," replied Nat; "but we form the society for debating, and therefore this ought to be the principal object. It may be well enough to have some declamations and dialogues occasionally—I think it would. But it will do us more good to debate. We shall be more interested in reading upon the subjects of debate, and then our debates will be better in consequence of our reading."

Tuesday evening arrived. Nat and his intimate associates had prepared a constitution, so that an organization could be effected without delay. A good number of young people assembled, of both sexes, and a society was formed in a most harmonious manner. The unanimity of feeling and action was a lesson to most legislative bodies, and to the Congress of the United States in particular. It was decided to hold weekly meetings for debate, and a question was voted for the meeting of the following week. Nat was appointed to open the discussion, and three others to follow on their respective sides of the question. A small fee of membership was required of the male members to defray necessary expenses.

"A good beginning last night," said Charlie to Nat, on the next morning.

"Much better than I anticipated," was Nat's reply. "The thing has taken better than I supposed it would; but many a good beginning has a bad ending. We must do our best to keep up the interest, and make it respectable."

"I was glad to hear you suggest that by-rule about good order," said Charlie. "I think some voted for it last evening who would not have done so if it had been deferred until disorder commenced."

"I knew what I was about," answered Nat. "There are some fellows in the village who would think they could have a good time in spite of the officers, because they are of the same age, and I thought it would be well to get them to vote for good order in the first place. We shall never accomplish any thing in such a society unless we have as much decorum as there is in the meetings of adults, and without it we shall have a bad reputation."

Here Nat exhibited one trait of his youth—a strong desire to make every thing in which he engaged respectable. A few years later he manifested a feeling in the same direction, when he was made captain of the fire company. He introduced rules to guard against those vices that are so likely to find their way into such associations; and his arguments were generally so good, and his appeals so forcible, that he always carried his propositions. The result was a model fire company that won the confidence and respect of the citizens. In his boyhood the same trait of character caused him to care for his appearance, so that in his poverty he was usually more neat and tidy in his dress than many sons of the rich with far costlier apparel. And it was this that had somewhat to do with the general manly character for which he was known when young.

"I suppose," continued Charlie, "that some men think we only mean to have a good time, and that there will be more play than profit in our society."

"And we must show them that it is otherwise by conducting it in the best way possible," added Nat. "For one, I want it for my own improvement. I had better stay at home and read than to go there and spend an evening to no advantage. Fellows who are not able to go to school, but must work from morning till night for a livelihood, are obliged to improve their odd moments if they would ever know any thing. You remember that rule of Dr. Franklin, 'Lose no time,' I suppose?"

"I can never forget Dr. Franklin where you are," answered Charlie. "You think he is law and gospel in every thing but the way to wealth."

The new-formed debating society filled the thoughts of Nat much of the time, and the first question for discussion was pretty thoroughly investigated before the time of the meeting. We do not know precisely what the question was, only that it was a common one, such as "Which is the greater curse to mankind, war or intemperance?" Suffice to say, that it was discussed on the evening appointed, in a manner that was creditable to all who participated, though the palm was readily conceded to Nat. The success of the first debate created a strong appetite for more, and from week to week the interest increased.

It happened one evening, for some reason, that no question was assigned for discussion. The members came, and a good number of spectators, but there was no provision made for a debate.

"What shall we do?" inquired Charlie, before the hour for opening the meeting arrived.

"Decide upon a question now, and, as soon as the meeting is opened, vote to discuss it," replied Nat, promptly.

"What! Do you mean to discuss it to-night?" asked John.

"To be sure I do. It would be a pretty joke to come together, and go home without doing any thing."

"I will agree to it," said Marcus.

"And I, too," said Frank.

"And I, too," added other voices.

So it was decided to have a discussion, and a question was agreed upon by the time the hour for commencing arrived. The meeting was opened, and the minutes of the last meeting read, when it appeared that there was no question for debate. Immediately Nat arose, and said, "Mr. President,—By some misunderstanding it appears that we have no question for discussion assigned for this evening. I think it would not be for our credit to go home without a debate, since those who have come here are expecting a discussion. I therefore move that we debate the following question this evening (at the same time reading the question), and that the President appoint the disputants as usual."

Frank seconded the motion, and it was carried. Next, the President appointed Nat to open the debate, and Marcus, Charlie, and Frank for the other three disputants. There was some curiosity on the part of spectators to see how the boys would get along, and they were all eager to have Nat begin. All looked very pleasant, however, and well they might, for who could view this young parliament scene without a smiling face. Still, it was possible to trace an anxious feeling upon the countenances of the debaters, unless we except Nat.

All other preliminary business being disposed of, Nat commenced, proceeded, and ended, in a speech of twenty minutes, that was not inferior to any of his previous performances. His speech had a beginning, middle, and end, and he stopped when he got through, which is not always the case even with some noted public speakers. The others followed, speaking about as well as usual, and gaining much applause to themselves. It was the general opinion, at the close of the evening, that there had not been a more interesting and profitable discussion in all their previous meetings.

"Nat, you was made for a debater," said Frank to him, at the close of the evening.

"That is a fact," added Charlie, who heard the remark. "You have superior abilities to examine and discuss a subject, and you command language as if you had studied the dictionary all your life. I suspect that pocket of yours holds the secret."

"No wonder that he takes such a stand," said Marcus, "he is always digging away for knowledge. I doubt if he has wasted a moment for five years. I am fully of the opinion, however, that uncommon abilities is the real cause of his success."

These tremendous compliments were flung directly into Nat's face, and he found it more difficult to reply than he did to speak on the unstudied question. At length he answered,

"You do not know me, boys. You overrate me. If I have any success in speaking, it is not because I have any greater abilities than you have. I have a taste for such discussions; I love to speak on the questions; and I desire to do it just as well as I can, and to improve upon it every week, and that is half the battle. I enter into it with all my soul, and don't stop to say I can't: that is all the difference."

"Pshaw, Nat! You will never make me believe that," said Charlie. "You don't believe it yourself. You are making the way to learning and eloquence as easy as Dr. Franklin's way to wealth, and I know what you think of that," and the roguish look that he cast upon him seemed to say, "I have you now."

"I say just what I believe," answered Nat. "The most eminent writers think that a person may be about what he determines to make himself, and I think it is true. If a man starts with the determination to be the best kind of a machinist or carpenter, he will ordinarily become so. And so if he is really determined to excel in any branch of knowledge, he will usually accomplish his object. Tell me of a great scholar or statesman who has not worked his way up by perseverance and incessant labor."

"All that may be very true," replied Marcus, "but it has nothing at all to do with the point in question. We do not say that the most gifted man will distinguish himself without improving his time by close application. We only say that one man is more highly endowed by nature than another."

"I admit that to a certain extent," answered Nat, "and still there is not so much truth in it as many people suppose. I really believe that if all the boys would set about improving every moment, as I have done for some years, you would not observe half so much difference in them as you do now."

The boys were rather unceremonious in piling such a load of compliments upon Nat. There were more than he could dispose of handily. Yet, the views which he advanced, and which he has always maintained from that time to this, are substantiated by the best authors we have. His views were essentially like those of Buxton, who said that he placed his confidence of success in "ordinary powers, and extraordinary application." Buxton's language, on one occasion, was very strong indeed upon the certain success of a firm purpose. "The longer I live," said he, "the more I am certain that the great difference between men, between the feeble and the powerful, is energy—invincible determination—a purpose once fixed, and then death or victory. That quality will do any thing that can be done in this world; and no talents, no circumstances, no opportunities will make a two-legged creature a man, without it." Here is a view of success exactly like that advanced by Nat to his companions; and other men, in the different callings of life, have expressed a similar opinion. Each youth must depend upon his own personal exertions, and not upon superior endowments, or wealthy or honored ancestry, for eminence. If his name is ever carved upon the temple of fame, he must carve it himself.

The debating society had a happy influence upon Nat. It called forth into exercise the latent powers of his mind that otherwise might have slept and slumbered. Such an organization has proved a valuable means of improvement to many persons in their early studies. The Irish orator, Curran, was indebted to such a "club" for much of the renown that attached to his after life. He was modest and retiring even to bashfulness, and had a very marked defect in his articulation, so that his schoolmates called him "stuttering Jack Curran." He joined a "debating club," determined to improve if possible, but there one of the first flings he received was to be called "Orator Mum," in consequence of his being so frightened when he arose to speak that he was not able to say a word. But he persevered until he became the champion of the "club," and laid the foundation of his future eminence as an orator. A living American statesman, who has already made his mark upon the land of his birth, considers the influence of a debating society to which he belonged in his youth, among the first stimulating causes of the course he has pursued. The highly distinguished English statesman, Canning, organized a House of Commons among his play-fellows at school, where a speaker was regularly elected, and ministerial and opposition parties were formed, and debates carried on, in imitation of Parliament. Canning became the star of this juvenile organization, and there began to develop those powers by which, a few years after, as another has said, "he ruled the House as a man rules the high-bred steed, as Alexander ruled Bucephalus, of whom it was said the horse and the rider were equally proud." Henry Clay, the American orator, said to some young men, "I owe my success in life chiefly to one circumstance,—that I commenced and continued for years the process of daily reading and speaking upon the contents of some historical or scientific book. These off-hand efforts were made, sometimes in a cornfield, at others in the forest, and not unfrequently in some distant barn, with the horse and ox for my auditors. It is to this early practice of the art of all arts that I am indebted for the primary and leading impulses that stimulated me onward, and have shaped and moulded my subsequent destiny." What speaking to the forest trees and beasts of the stall was to Clay, that was the debating society to Nat. It was a place where he could use the knowledge he acquired by reading, while, at the same time, his mind was stimulated to action, so that he began to utter "thoughts that breathe and words that burn."

Some twelve or fourteen years ago, the author was passing Tremont Temple in Boston, when he observed an illuminated sign over the door of one of its basement rooms, "Boston Young Men's Total Abstinence Society," and in connection with it was a most cordial "Walk In." We accepted the silent invitation, and entered. There we found a few young men engaged in a debate, and some five or six spectators, among whom was Deacon Grant, listening. After the close of the exercises, the young men came forward in a most cordial and genial way to converse, and I learned that they had a small library, and were accustomed to debate questions of a social and literary character at their meetings. Only a few belonged to the society; for it has always been true that total abstinence societies have not been well supported in Boston, and the fact is a stain upon its social character, and the piety of its churches; but those few were anxious to make the society a means of mental improvement, at the same time it contributed to prosper the cause of temperance. For some years the organization was conducted in this way; and what was the result? We are not able to point to all the members as they now meet the stern duties of meridian life, but we know the whereabouts and position of a few. One of them, who was a mason by trade, at the time referred to above, is the popular editor of a daily paper in a New England city, and his charming eloquence has more than once delighted a Boston audience. Another has worked his way along through a course of education, and now occupies an honorable position as a preacher of the gospel. Yet another applied himself to self-improvement with industry and perseverance, and the world know him now as the talented author, Oliver Optics. And still another, a merchant's clerk, now stands at the head of the large mercantile house in which he then served, possessing wealth and position that many an older man would be proud to call his own. His beautiful city mansion contains a study, where leisure hours are profitably employed, showing that the stimulus of those early debates is still felt. His voice is often heard in public assemblies, and he now takes his turn, with a corps of divines and lawyers, in editing a religious magazine. Not one of these young men had wealth, or titled ancestry, or superior advantages, to aid them; and all will say that the debates of their society exerted a powerful influence over them, and contributed largely to their success.

CHAPTER XIX.

COMING AND GOING.

Frank was much surprised one day to receive a visit from Ben Drake.

"Is it you, Ben?" he exclaimed, as he met him at the door.

"I believe it is," said Ben, "though I hope I am a different Ben from what I was five years ago," evidently retaining some recollection of Trip's death.

"I should not have known you," said Frank, "if I had passed you in the street. How you have grown!"

Frank had really no better opinion of Ben now than he had when Trip was tumbled down Prospect Hill, and he was sorry to see him coming up to his father's door. Still, he was so much improved in his appearance, and he met Frank so much more gentlemanly than he ever did before, that the latter could not but give him a cordial welcome.

"You have changed as much as I have, I think," added Ben, "though, in one respect, there was not so much room for a change in your case as there was in mine." But this allusion Frank did not comprehend.

"Come in, come in," said Frank, and he ushered him into the house, where he met the family, who were rather surprised to see him. Mrs. Martin made inquiries after the family, to which Ben responded in a manner that evidenced great improvement.

"Where do you live?" she asked.

"I am now at school in Andover."

"Ah! you have better advantages than the rest of the boys."

"And I hope I improve them better than I used to," said Ben. "I was a pretty wild boy when I lived here, and it has caused me many regrets."

"How long are you going to school?" inquired Mrs. Martin.

"I expect to prepare for college there."

"You do? Then you are going to have a liberal education? What are you going to be,—a lawyer?"

"No; I hope to do more good than I could to be a lawyer. I expect to be a minister."

Frank and his mother were both surprised at this announcement, and the latter asked,

"Then you are a Christian?"

"I trust I am. Nothing but becoming a Christian could have saved me from my wicked ways."

"How long since you became a Christian?"

"It is eight or ten months."

Other inquiries elicited the fact, that his brother Sam was no better than when he left town, and that much of the time his parents knew nothing of his whereabouts.

As the evening drew on (Frank had invited Ben to stay with him), Ben inquired if there was a prayer-meeting on that evening, to which he received an affirmative answer.

"Will you go?" he asked, addressing himself to Frank.

"Yes; if you wish to have me. It will soon be time to go."

They went to the prayer-meeting, and entered the room just as the exercises commenced. A good number were present, some of whose faces Ben recognized, though scarcely any one at first knew him. In the course of the evening he arose and spoke in a feeling way of his own experience, referred to his former recklessness in that village, and disclosed his purpose to become a minister of Christ. Before he sat down, most of those present recognized the once bad boy, and they were both surprised and delighted. Frank could hardly believe what he saw and heard. He never expected that Ben Drake would take such a stand as this; and he thought much, but said little.

Early the next morning, Frank ran over to inform Nat of the arrival of Ben, and the fact that he was going to make a minister.

"Going to be a minister!" exclaimed Nat. "I should like to know what can be found in him to make a minister of."

"Well, he is certainly in the school at Andover, preparing for college,—if he tells the truth,—and you have no idea how much improved he is."

"He is deceiving you, Frank. I have no confidence in the fellow. He always was bad, and he always will be."

"No; he is pious now. I went to the prayer-meeting with him last night, and he spoke. He spoke well, too, and alluded to his evil ways when he lived here, and expressed much regret at his course."

"I can scarcely believe it," replied Nat, "though I used to think that Ben would not be so bad if Sam was out of the way. What has become of Sam? There is not much danger of his becoming pious, I take it."

"Ben is not inclined to talk very freely about him, but from what we have learned, the family don't know where he is much of the time."

"How long is it since Ben reformed?"

"Only eight or ten months. Mother says he appears well now, but she would rather wait to see how he holds out. She is afraid that his early vicious habits will be too strong for his present good purpose."

"Where is he now?" inquired Nat, becoming intensely interested in the case. "Is he not coming around to see us?"

"Yes; he will go about some to-day, and go home to-morrow."

Ben called upon many of his old acquaintances that day, so that they had an opportunity of seeing him, and all were as much surprised as Frank at the change in his appearance. His visit created quite a sensation in a circle of families, where he was particularly known in his early boyhood, and he was the occasion of many remarks after his departure. Hereafter we shall see what kind of a man he made.

Before the young people had fairly recovered from the surprise occasioned by Ben's visit, news came that Daniel Webster was to speak in Faneuil Hall, Boston, on a certain evening.

"I shall go to hear him," said Nat, as soon as he heard of it. "Will you go, Charlie?"

"How will you go?" asked Charlie.

"With my own team, of course," answered Nat, jestingly.

"And walk home after the address?"

"Certainly; there is no other way for we poor fellows to do. I never heard Daniel Webster speak, and I shall hear him if it is a possible thing. Will you go?"

"Yes, I will," answered Charlie. "You are not to have all the glory of walking to Boston. I will try it for once."

"*I* expect to try it a good many times," said Nat. "I want to hear some of the orators of whom so much is said. There is much to be learned in watching a speaker, and listening to him. His manners teach as well as his thoughts. I intend to hear Edward Everett the first time he speaks within ten or fifteen miles of here."

"I see what you are after," said Charlie. "You mean to discover the secret of their power, if possible, and I hope you will."

On the evening of Webster's speech, Nat and Charlie were on their way to Boston in good season, and arrived at Faneuil Hall before the hour for the meeting. They hurried in to find eligible seats before the hall was crowded. Many were already there, and many more were constantly coming in. Nat found that he could see the speaker better to stand directly in front of the platform, where many were already awaiting the arrival of the great orator. So there he took his place, with Charlie by his side, forgetting that his limbs were weary with the ten miles' walk, and a day's hard toil in the machine-shop.

Hearty cheers announced the arrival of the orator, whom Nat had not seen before, and still another round of applause went up when he arose to speak. It was a great treat for Nat to listen to the man whose fame made his name familiar to every school-boy. He drank in every word of his speech, closely observed every gesture and modulation of voice, and would have sat entranced till morning, "taking no note of time," if the gifted orator had continued to pour forth his eloquence.

"Could any thing be grander than that?" said Nat, as they were leaving the house. "I would walk twice as far to hear another speech like it."

"It was very fine indeed," answered Charlie. "It far exceeded my expectations, high as my hopes were raised."

"What power there is in the human voice to control men!" said Nat. "How still it was in the hall! You could almost hear a pin drop, they were so chained by his eloquence. What else could hold them so long in such silence!"

"Nothing," replied Charlie. "It has given me a new idea of eloquence altogether. His voice alone, without a thought, is enough to command attention."

"I could but notice his choice of language," added Nat; "every word seemed to be the most expressive one he could find, and some of his gestures appeared to make his words mean much more than they really do."

Nat had always been a close observer of public speakers from his boyhood, and lost no opportunity to hear lecturers who came to his native village. At the time he heard Webster, his desire to listen to the leading orators of the day had developed almost into a passion. The Debating Society had probably sharpened his taste for such intellectual treats, and he was fully resolved to hear all the speakers he could. He seldom left his book in the evening, except to hear some public speaker at home and abroad, or to debate a question in the club. Many times he walked into Boston to listen to some distinguished orator, returning, often alone, after the treat was enjoyed. This was the pains he took to hear Edward Everett several times, who became his favorite. He admired him for the elegance of his diction, and the beauty with which all of his addresses were invested. He saw more power in Webster, and more elegance in Everett.

He frequently walked into neighboring towns to hear lectures and political speeches. A good speaker announced anywhere in the vicinity was sure to call him out, whether the speech was upon education or politics. One great object with him seemed to be, to learn the art of oratory by actual observation. It is probably true, that he acquired more knowledge of the English language by listening to gifted speakers than he ever did from books, and more of the true art of using it himself to sway an audience. It is said that Robert Bloomfield, when a poor boy, having only a newspaper and an old English dictionary with which to gratify his thirst for information, acquired a very good knowledge of pronunciation by listening to the clerical orator, Mr. Fawcet. Drawn by the speaker's popularity, he went to hear him one Sabbath evening, and he was so impressed with his choice and enunciation of words, that he continued to attend his preaching in order to perfect himself in the proper use of language
—not a very high object for which to hear preaching, but illustrative of what may be learned by close observation. In this way Nat, like Bloomfield and Patrick Henry, studied "men and things," in connection with books, during the eventful years of his apprenticeship.

Nat's admiration of the power of the human voice was not all a youthful hallucination. What is there like it? From the nursery to the Senate it controls and sways the heart of man. From the mother's voice at the fireside, to the eloquence of a Webster in the "cradle of liberty," it soothes, arouses, elevates, or depresses, at its pleasure. Listen to the gifted orator, as the flowing periods come burning from his soul on fire, riveting the attention of his hearers in breathless silence for an hour, almost causing them to feel what he feels, and to believe what he believes, and bearing them upward by the witchery of his lofty eloquence until they scarcely know whether they are in the flesh or not, and say if there is aught of earth to compare with the power of the human voice.

CHAPTER XX.

GOSSIP.

One such youth as Nat in a country village is the occasion of a good deal of gossip. Many opinions are expressed in regard to his motives and prospects, though in this case there were few conflicting sentiments. In the sewing circle, a good old lady, who could not appreciate education because she had none herself, said,

"Nat is a smart feller, but I'm feared he'll never be nothin' he thinks so much of book larning. I 'spose he thinks he can get a living by his wits."

The old lady had a half dozen champions of the tongue down upon her at once.

"No, no, Mrs. Lane," said one, "you judge Nat too severely. There is no one who attends to his work more closely than he does. You never heard one of his employers complain that he was indifferent to his business."

"He only employs his leisure moments in study," said another; "and I think that is much to his credit. If more boys in the village were like him, it would be vastly to our credit, and theirs, too."

"Yes," added a third; "and you may be sure that when a boy is reading during his evenings, and at other spare moments, he is out of mischief, and that is something in these days. There are parents in this town who never know that their sons are spending their leisure time well, because they are so often getting into bad scrapes. I guess if we could look into the tavern some evenings, we should find some of them there smoking and drinking."

"Wall," replied the old lady, "that may all be true enough, but too many edicated men are worse than none at all."

"Not if they earn their living, as Nat does, and get an education into the bargain," said one of the former speakers. "There is no danger that our sons and daughters will know too much. Most of them are satisfied with knowing too little."

"Wall, edication is good enough in its place," added Mrs. Lane, "but what does Nat 'spect to do with it in the machine-shop? You won't make me b'lieve that larning is good for anybody who will have no use for it. 'Spose a farmer studies the lor, what good will it do him if he only farms it? It will do him more hurt than good, because he will be nuther one thing nor 'tother. If we have farmers, let's have farmers, and if we have machinists, let's have machinists."

"Perhaps Nat will not always work at his trade," suggested one of the company. "There are many self-made men who are now serving society much better than they would be if they had continued to work at manual labor."

"Yis, that's it," exclaimed the old lady, with some earnestness; "that is jist what it will come to. These boys who take so to book larning will stop working soon as they b'lieve they can get their bread and butter by their wits. That's jist what I meant in the fust place. I hear 'um tell that Nat goes to Boston nights to hear some great speakers, and comes home afterwards, and I thinks it is ventersome. I'd never let a son of mine do it, in this world."

"Why? why?" inquired two or three voices at once.

"Why? a good reason why. You never know'd a boy who can be trusted in Boston nights. You don't know where they'll go to, and if ye do, there are sharpers on the lookout to lead them into evil. And who knows but robbers might seize him on his way back? I should think the boy was crazy."

"It is only an illustration of his energy and perseverance, Mrs. Lane," said one of the ladies. "He is determined to know something, though he has no time to learn except in his leisure hours; and it is really surprising how much a person may acquire by industry in these fragments of time."

"There's a nuther thing, too," continued Mrs. Lane. "I hear 'um tell that Nat carts a book about in his pocket all the time he works. Pretty business, I think, for a youngster like him to try to be a scholar and worker at once! It's all proof to me that taking to books so will spile him for anything."

"One thing is certain, Mrs. Lane, that he does not mean to waste any time; for the book in his pocket is to take out when he has a minute to spare. If he gets only ten minutes in a day to read, that will be one hour in the six working days, which is worth saving. That single hour a day, in a lifetime, would give a man considerable knowledge."

"Wall, it's no use arguing about it. Times are so diff'rent now from what they was when I was young, and peoples thinks so diff'rent, that it 'pears to me sometimes that the world is going to rack and ruin. We got along well 'nough fifty or sixty years ago without so much edication. But folks are got to be so stylish now, and boys know so much more than their grandpas, that I railly don't know what'll come on us."

"After all, Mrs. Lane, I think you would rather have more boys like Nat, than like some others I could name," said a former speaker.

"Lor, yis," she replied; "I guess I should. I allers liked Nat. He's a rale clever feller as ever lived, and he ain't stuck-up by his smartness, and he likes to see everybody well used. I larfed myself most to death when I heard about his waitin' on Hanner Mann to the party. It's jist like Nat, he can't bear to see anybody slighted."

"I like to see that," answered one of the number; "it is a good sign. He thought Hannah and her sister were slighted because their father was poor and intemperate, and they were not able to dress quite so well as some others, and this excited his sympathies, so that he was determined they should go to the party."

"I know'd all about that," replied Mrs. Lane, "and that's what pleased me so, to see a youngster like him so inderpendent, and stand up for good folks if they are poor."

The reference here to an incident of Nat's youthful experience needs explanation, as the fact illustrates an element of his character from childhood, and furnishes additional reason for the course in which his sympathies and better feelings ran thereafter. Nat and Charlie had received invitations to a social gathering, in connection with their companions, and the following conversation and decision occurred with reference to attending.

"There is Hannah Mann, and her sister," said Nat, "they never go. Nobody thinks they are good enough to associate with them, because they are poor and unable to dress as well as some others."

"I have observed it," answered Charlie. "Some of the girls are always making sport of them, and I doubt if any of the fellows ever waited upon them. Yet they are as good as the best of them, for aught I know."

"That is true," added Nat; "they appear well, and are good scholars, and know twice as much as some of the girls who slight them. A splendid silk dress would not improve their characters at all, though it might their personal appearance. I will tell you what I will do, Charlie; if you will wait upon one of them, I will upon the other. What do you say to it?"

"I say amen to it," answered Charlie. "They are as good as I am any day, and I ought not to endanger the characters of those who are better by going with them."

"I am in earnest. I mean just what I say," continued Nat.

"So am I in earnest," said Charlie, smiling. "Did you think I am joking?"

"I thought you looked rather unbelieving, as if you imagined *I* was jesting."

"No such thing; your proposition rather pleased me than otherwise."

"Well, then," said Nat, "it is settled that we go to the party, and wait upon these girls, is it?"

"Certainly, if you say so."

This decision was carried out. The two sisters were escorted to the party by Nat and Charlie, to the surprise of some of the better apparelled girls, who were secretly hoping to be the fortunate ones themselves. The incident created quite a sensation among the young people. At first, they did not quite understand it; but they were not long in discovering that Nat intended to rebuke their ungenerous treatment of these girls. Some were inclined to exhibit a little resentment; but they soon perceived that it would only make a bad matter worse. Nat "laughed behind his ears" to see how the thing worked, and many a knowing glance was exchanged with Charlie in the course of the evening. Before sun-down, on the following day, the facts in the case were known by many of the villagers. The aristocratic ones sneered at the act, while others commended it as the fruit of a generous spirit. On the whole, it did much good in the community, because it caused many persons to see the unkindness and even cruelty of slighting the worthy, on account of their humble origin and circumstances.

That decision and independence, which aided Nat so much in his studies, enabled him to perform this act. An irresolute, dull, stupid, inefficient youth, would not have braved the current of feeling that had set against the girls. In this way it is, that the leading elements of character hitherto discussed assist a youth in all circumstances. He is more of a man in doing both little and great things. They dignify common politeness as really as they do achievements in art and science. They make the gentleman as truly as the scholar. Robert Burns was once walking in the streets of Edinburgh, in company with an aristocratic associate, when the latter rebuked him for stopping to speak to a rough but worthy farmer who had come to market, and Burns' reply evinced just the spirit which Nat admired. "Why, you fantastic gomeral," said he, "it was not the great coat, the scone bonnet, and the saunders boots hose that I spoke to, but *the man* that was in them; and the man, sir, for true worth, would weigh down you and me, and ten more such, any day."

CHAPTER XXI.

GOING TO THE THEATRE.

Nat had become an admirer of Shakspeare's dramatic works, and hour after hour he read them with increasing interest. The more he studied them, the more he saw to admire. He had never seen one of them acted on the stage, and, in connection with the displays of eloquence to which he had been a witness of late, he became desirous of witnessing a theatrical performance. To heighten his interest, he saw it announced that the elder Booth would perform in Boston on a given night. He resolved to go.

"Marcus," said he, "did you know that Booth is to perform at the theatre in Boston on Monday night?"

"No," answered Marcus, "is it so?"

"It is so announced in the papers, and I think I shall go."

"And walk?" inquired Marcus.

"Yes; I can walk there as well as to walk to Faneuil Hall to hear Webster and Everett."

"You won't get home till morning."

"I can get home by one o'clock, and possibly before. I wish *you* would go, and Frank and Charlie."

"I will go if they will," answered Marcus. "I should like to see a tragedy acted for once."

"It is said that Booth is one of the best readers and speakers of Shakspeare," continued Nat, "and I want to hear him. He is a great imitator, and personates the different characters exactly. I don't feel that I know how to read Shakspeare very well; perhaps I can learn something about it from him."

It was decided to consult Frank and Charlie, and secure their company if possible. Both of them yielded to the proposition, though Charlie suggested,

"That many people would think they were hurrying to ruin if they should hear of their going."

"Perhaps they will," said Nat, "and I have no doubt that many persons have been ruined by going; but they did not go for the same object that we go. I am not going just for the pleasure of witnessing the play, by any means; I want to see how the actors personate the different characters. To read Shakspeare well, it must be read just as it is spoken."

"No one will stop to consider your motive in going, nor mine," said Charlie. "They think that the theatre is a bad place, and see not why it will ruin one and not another."

"Well, I shall do as I think it is best for myself," answered Nat, in that spirit of independence and self-reliance for which he was known; "I shall go once to see, and if I think I can learn any thing to my advantage, I shall go again, and stop when I have obtained what I want."

"That's cool enough," said Frank; "you would make a good refrigerator in dog-days. Perhaps you intend to be an actor?"

"No, I don't fancy the business. I shall be satisfied to *see* one."

Some of their friends propounded objections to this project, but they were overruled by a full and clear statement of their object in going. Then, too, the general good character which they bore, and their usual prudence in avoiding bad company, combined to remove more easily all the objections propounded.

The evening of the entertainment was pleasant, and it was indeed a new step for them, as we see them standing at the entrance of the theatre. To how many it has been the turning point of life! "Entrance to the Pit," they read in capitals, with a hand pointing thither,—and to how many it has been emphatically *the entrance to the pit*, in a most appalling sense! It was a hazardous experiment for Nat and his companions,—even more dangerous than the attempt to swim four rods under water. But they entered with the multitude who were pouring in, drawn thither by the popularity of the actor announced. The play commenced, and scene after scene passed before the eyes of Nat, every word of which he had read over and over again; but now, for the first time, he beheld the characters in living persons. To him it was putting the breath of life into what was before beautiful but dead. The play that was classic and charming to read, was now human-like and wonderful to act. There was more force, meaning, and power in the text than he had ever attached to it,—much as he had loved to read it. Closely he observed the distinguished actor, noticing the utterance of every word, and the significance of every gesture and motion, with sharp discrimination, until he almost felt that he could do the like himself. It was a memorable evening to Nat, and language could scarcely express all he thought and felt.

"Nat, you will like Shakspeare better than ever now, will you not?" said Charlie.

"More than that," replied Nat. "It seems to me I never understood that play before. I was reading it the other day, but it is so much more grand when spoken and acted, that I should hardly know it.”

“Did you observe the bar when you was coming out?” inquired Frank, addressing himself to Marcus.

“Yes, and I thought by the appearance they did quite a business in the line of drinking.”

“They always have bars in theatres,” said Nat, “and that is one reason why they lead persons to ruin. No doubt many are drawn there as much by the bar as they are by the play.”

“What is the reason they can’t have a theatre without having such vices connected with it?” inquired Charlie.

“Because they don’t try,” answered Nat. “I suppose that theatres are generally managed by men who are in favor of drinking, and they would not shut out such things of course. I think that men of principle might establish one that would be unobjectionable; for they would allow no such evils to be harbored there.”

“Perhaps you can get Parson Fiske and Deacon White to get one up,” said Marcus, laughing at Nat’s suggestion, “and then you won’t have to walk ten miles and back to witness a play.”

“Ten miles or not,” said Nat, “I have been well paid to-night. There is a great deal to be learned in witnessing one such performance. I can read Shakspeare now with more interest and profit than ever. I want to hear ‘The Tempest’ played now, and ‘King Lear,’ and ‘Hamlet,’ and ‘Romeo and Juliet,’ and I mean to the first chance I have.”

“Ah, Nat,” said Charlie, “I see that it is a foregone conclusion with you,—you are half ruined now—the more you have, the more you want. We shall be obliged to look after him more closely,” addressing the last sentence to Marcus and Frank.

“Yes,” added Marcus, “by the time he has heard all these plays, he will be patronizing that bar, and we shall see him reported in the Police Court in the morning.”

By the time the clock struck one, Nat was at home. His visit to the theatre was not kept secret. It was soon quite generally known that he had been to the theatre, and many remarks were elicited by the fact. Good people did not respect theatres more at that time than they do now, so that they regarded this step of Nat as taken in the wrong direction.

“I am afraid that all the hopes Nat has raised among his friends will be dashed now,” said one. “When a youth gets to going to the theatre, there is little hope of his doing well. I hardly thought this of him."

"I thought Nat always wanted things respectable," said a gentleman. "Does he consider the theatre a respectable place?"

"What has he done with his books?" inquired another. "I supposed that he thought of little but an education,—does he find the theatre a good school in which to be educated?"

"It is a good school in which to be educated for evil," replied the individual to whom the remark was addressed.

One person, however, was heard to say,

"It will not hurt Nat at all. You may be sure that he did not go there just for the pleasure of the thing. I have no doubt that he went for the same reason that he went to hear Webster, Everett, and others speak,—to learn something. He was drawn thither, not by his love of amusement, but by his desire to learn. Nat learns more by seeing, than half the scholars do by hard study."

"What in the world could he learn there that is good?" inquired a person who heard the last remark.

"He could learn how to speak better, if nothing else," was the reply. "And *that* he said, in the beginning, was his object in going. When he has acquired what he thinks he can get there to aid him, you will see that he will stop."

"And by that time he may be ruined," was the reply.

Nat carried out his resolution, and went to the theatre a number of times, to hear certain plays, walking to Boston and back each time. One result of his visits was to increase his interest in Shakspeare, so that he began to practise reading his plays aloud, and personating the different characters. He made decided progress in this art, and subsequently gave public readings of Shakspeare, by which he gained much applause. The result satisfied nearly every one, that he went to the theatre simply to observe the manner of speaking, as he went to hear distinguished orators.

That the object for which a youth visits the theatre will decide, in a great measure, its influence upon him, no one can deny, and it is so with all forms of amusement. If he is drawn thither by the fascination of the play alone, yielding himself up to the witchery of it, without any regard to the intellectual or moral character of the scenic representations, he is in a dangerous path. A large majority of those who visit the theatre with this motive, as mere thoughtless pleasure-lovers, are probably ruined.

The youthful reader should not infer that it is altogether safe to visit the theatre, even for the reason that Nat did. It was a hazardous step for him on account of the attractions that are thrown around it to dazzle and bewilder. A high aim, in the path of knowledge, and great energy and decision of character to execute his purpose, were his protection. Perhaps not ten of a hundred youth could do the same thing, and be saved from ruin. Augustine tells of a Christian young man who was prevailed upon to visit the amphitheatre to witness the gladiatorial games. He was unfriendly to such sports, and consented to go solely to please his companion. For his own protection he resolved to close his eyes that he might not be influenced by the scene. For some time he kept his eyes closed; but, at length, a tremendous shout caused him to open them, and look out upon the arena. In an instant, he was fired with the spirit of those around him,—he cheered the gladiators on,

—he shouted with all his might,—and ever after he became a constant patron of the games. So it is often with the youth, in our day, who goes to the theatre *for once* only. He merely wants to see what the theatre is, resolved, perhaps, that he will never be known as a theatre-goer. But he cannot withstand the fascination. Once going has created an irresistible desire to go again, and again, and again, until his character is ruined. Where one derives the impulse and knowledge that Nat did, a hundred are destroyed. It is not wise, then, to try the experiment. It is acquiring knowledge at too great a risk. Who would cross a rough and stormy river where he knew that only one in a hundred had reached the other shore?

Theatres have always been schools of vice. There never was a time when their influence was good. At the time our country was struggling for independence, Congress passed an act recommending the different States to suppress theatrical performances by law; and soon after they passed another act declaring that no person who visited the theatre should hold an office under the government. It seems impossible to make them otherwise than disreputable. Attempts have been made to establish *respectable* theatres, but they have always failed. Such an attempt was made to reform one of the royal theatres of London, some years ago, and the committee to whom the subject was submitted reported that the institution could not be supported after such reform. The experiment was actually tried with the late Tremont Theatre, in Boston. Intoxicating drinks were not allowed to be sold, and no females were admitted unaccompanied by gentlemen, as the better class of people would not attend if profligate persons were admitted. But the theatre could not be supported on these principles, and the plan was abandoned. A report was published, in which it was stated, that if the rent of the building was free, it could not be sustained by the reform system. Intemperance and licentiousness appear to be indispensable to support the theatre. There is good reason, then, for the legend recorded by Tertullian, running as follows: A Christian woman went to the theatre, and came home possessed of a demon. Her confessor, seeking to cast out the evil one, demanded of him how he dared to take possession of a believer, who, by holy baptism, had been redeemed out of his kingdom. "I have done nothing but what is proper," said the devil, "for I found her on my own territory." He might have made a captive of Nat for the same reason.

Some pronounce this hostility to theatres a prejudice of Christian ministers and their sympathizers, but this is not true. The popular actor, Macready, who won a world-wide fame in the business, by his long connection with the stage, expressed a similar opinion of theatres after he left the play. He settled in Sherbourne, England, where he had a pleasant, promising family, and one rule to which his children were subjected was, "None of my children shall ever, with my consent or on any pretence, enter a theatre, or have any visiting connection with actors and actresses." The honored Judge Bulstrode at one time expressed the feelings of the English bench, when, in his charge to the grand jury of Middlesex, he said, "One play-house ruins more souls than fifty churches are able to save." Sir Matthew Hale relates that when he was at Oxford, he was making rapid advancement in his studies when the stage-players came thither, and he went to the performance, and became so corrupted that he almost entirely forsook his studies. He was saved only by resolving never to attend another play. Even the infidel, Rousseau, condemned theatres. He said, "I observe that the situation of an actor is a state of licentiousness and bad morals; that the men are abandoned to disorder; that the women lead a scandalous life; that the one and the other, at once avaricious and profane, ever overwhelmed with debt, and ever prodigal, are as unrestrained in their dissipation as they are void of scruple in respect to the means of providing for it. In all countries their profession is dishonorable; those who exercise it are everywhere contemned."

CHAPTER XXII.

THE DRAMATIC SOCIETY.

"Let us form a dramatic society," said Nat to his companions, one day. "Perhaps we can put an extra touch on 'Henry the Eighth' or 'The Merchant of Venice.'"

"I should laugh," answered Charlie, "to see us undertaking the drama. I guess it would be straining at a *gnat* (Nat) and swallowing a camel," attempting to perpetrate a pun, over which he, at whose expense it was said, laughed as heartily as any of them.

"Let Charlie laugh as much as he pleases," said Marcus, "I think we could do well in such an enterprise. We might not eclipse Booth, but we could get along without a bar and some other things as bad."

"You will find," continued Charlie, "that a play of Shakspeare will not go off very well without scenery."

"Of course it would not," replied Nat. "But we must have scenery of some kind."

"Where will you get it?"

"Make it," quickly responded Nat. "It will be an easy matter to paint such representations as will answer our purpose."

"So you will turn actor and artist all at once," said Charlie. "What will you try to do next, Nat?"

"As to that," answered Nat, "I will let you know when I have done this. 'One thing at a time,' was Dr. Franklin's rule. But say, now, will you all enlist for a dramatic society?"

Frank and Marcus replied promptly in the affirmative, and Charlie brought up the rear, by saying,

"Well, I suppose I must be on the popular side, and go with the majority—yea."

Here was one of the fruits of going to the theatre. What had been witnessed there created the desire to undertake the same, although Nat's object was to improve himself in rhetorical exercises. But the enterprise grew out of his visits to the theatre, and was well suited to excite critical remarks. It is probable that most actors and actresses are made so by first witnessing theatrical performances. We are acquainted with a person, whose nephew is an actor, with no purer character than actors usually possess. He was a lover of books in his youth; and his desire to become an actor was begotten in the theatre. He was so delighted with what he saw on the stage, that he finally resolved to make stage-playing his profession; and he now belongs to that unhonored fraternity. It is not strange that some people were surprised that Nat should originate such a society.

"What shall we play?" inquired Frank, on the evening the dramatic society was organized.

"'Macbeth,'" replied Nat, who had witnessed this at the theatre. "It may be more difficult than some others, but it is one of the best plays."

"*You* must get up the scenery," said Frank.

"With the assistance of the rest of you," replied Nat. "It will be no great affair to paint what we want for this play."

"How long will it take?" inquired Marcus.

"We can do it in two evenings," answered Nat. "We ought not to be longer than that, if we intend to commit the play so as to act it nextweek."

"No one but members of the society will be admitted, I suppose," said Charlie, "until we have thoroughly practised the play."

"No; we must speak it over and over, so that it will be perfectly familiar, before we attempt it before visitors."

On that evening the society was organized by the choice of officers and the adoption of a constitution and by-laws. Nat had the chief agency in preparing the constitution and by-laws, as he did in the debating society, and he found that a knowledge of grammar was indeed a decided assistance. He was often reminded of the remarks of his teacher, when he (Nat) was opposed to studying the science.

It was decided to act "Macbeth," and the parts were assigned, and the time of the first meeting appointed. Many of the young people joined the society, and were much interested in its object. Such an organization was suited to awaken more enthusiasm among the young, than a debating society.

It was a pleasant evening on which the play was to be performed for the first time, and every member of the society was there, curious to behold the result. It went off with considerable eclat, although there were some blunders and mistakes, as might have been expected. Even Charlie, who was incredulous about their success, confessed that it passed off very well. The scenery, which had been prepared by the boys, under Nat's direction, was quite decent, and it showed that Nat's early practice of drawing was very useful to him now. It would not bear very close inspection, it is true; but a short distance off, and by lamp-light, it looked very well.

Thus evening after evening they met, with closed doors, to practise the piece. At length, concluding that they could entertain an audience, they decided upon a public performance. The plan was adopted with much spirit, and all were resolved to do their best.

The entertainment was given at the appointed time, and a good audience assembled. Each one performed his part well, but Nat, as usual, was thought to excel.

"I had no idea the boys would do so well," said Mr. Graves. "I am surprised that Nat should perform so handsomely; he would make a complete actor with practice."

"Marcus did very well indeed," replied the gentleman to whom he addressed the remark; "in fact, all of them exceeded my expectations. But Nat plays as if he were perfectly at home."

"I don't know about the influence of such things," added Mr. Graves. "I have my fears that such a society will foster a love for theatrical exhibitions of a far more exceptionable character."

"I feel exactly so, too. I think it may lead some of the young people here to attend the theatre, when otherwise they would not. There is no doubt that Nat originated this society in consequence of attending the theatre himself. If nothing worse than such an exhibition as we have had to-night would grow out of it, it would be well enough. I would say amen to it. But I fear that it will lead to something else."

"There is the danger," replied Mr. G. "Young people are easily led astray by such appeals to their senses, and the more easily because they do not see any evil in them. It is just as it is with using intoxicating drinks. A young man sees no wrong in sipping a little wine at a party; but that first wine-glass may create an appetite that will make him a drunkard. So the sight of such a theatrical performance as this may lead some of the boys to want to witness a play on a grander scale at the theatre."

The exhibition of the Dramatic Society occasioned many remarks like the above in the village. Some people had expressed their opinions unfavorably before the exhibition, but this settled the matter in their view. The very skill which the boys displayed in the performance served to awaken still greater fears; for the greater the witchery of the play, the more danger to the young.

"Thar," said old Mrs. Lane, who entertained us on a former occasion, "I knowd that it would turn out so. It is jist what I telled ye, when I heard Nat went to Boston nights arter great speakers. You'll have to b'lieve me byme bye whether or no."

"Ah!" said the lady addressed, "it would all have been well enough if Nat had confined his attention to that. Perhaps it will be well enough now, though I fear that theatrical performances will have a bad influence."

"Pesky bad," replied the old lady. "When boys are runnin arter such things allers, there is no tellin whar they'll stop. And thar's the danger of too much edication. If Nat had stuck to his bobbin, and never knowd any thing else, I guess it would turn out better for him in the eend. I don't b'lieve in so many new-fangled notions as they have in these ere times."

"I have no fears for Nat," responded the lady; "for I think he participates in these things for self-improvement; but others may do it for the sake of the amusement. I am afraid that others may imbibe a taste for the drama, and become theatre-goers in consequence."

"You seem to think that Nat can't be spiled; but I take it that his good motives can't make the theatre good. It is a corruptious place, anyhow, and if it don't spile him, it won't be because it ain't bad enough."

"Time will show us the result," continued the lady. "But they say Nat exhibited marked talents for the drama at the exhibition. Several persons have told me that they were surprised at his ability, but I am not; for he always excels in whatever he undertakes. He enters into every thing with all his heart, and does it with all his might."

"Lor, yes, we all know that," replied Mrs. Lane; "and so I reckon that if the theatre should spile him, he would be wicked with all his might. He'd make a rale prodergal son, only more so."

On the point of Nat's excellence in performing the drama, the following conversation took place after this public entertainment.

"You ought to be an actor," said Charlie to him. "You are exactly cut out for it, and every one who heard you the other night would tell you so."

"So far as that is concerned," answered Nat, "the profession of an actor is the last one I should choose."

"Why?" inquired Charlie. "I thought you was in love with the business."

"By no means. I have told you over and over my object in going to the theatre, and in forming the Dramatic Society, but you always appear to doubt me. I would not be an actor even if I could be as famous as Booth."

"You would not? and yet many seem to think you have a taste in that direction, and *I* have thought so too. But tell me why not."

"Because I have little respect for the business as a profession. It affords a brief pleasure to an audience for a short time, and that is all it amounts to. I think it is a good discipline for us in the Dramatic Society, and I know that I learned some valuable lessons at the theatre, and I am still of the opinion that a theatre might be so conducted as to prove a source of innocent amusement, and not a curse."

"You couldn't make many of the people in this community believe that," said

Charlie. "They think it is a gone case with you since you have favored theatricals."

"I know that," replied Nat, "and they would not believe me if I should tell them what I have you, so that I see no way to convince them but to wait, and time will do it. I would carry bobbin all my life before I would be an actor."

"Well, what would you be, Nat, if you could have your own way?" inquired Charlie.

"I would be an orator and statesman like Edward Everett," quickly answered Nat. "I always had great respect for such men. It is easy to respect them; but no man can cherish high respect for an actor."

Here the conversation was interrupted.

CHAPTER XXIII.

THE SURPRISE.

"Heard the news, Nat?" inquired Frank one morning.

"No, what is it?"

"The men are going to annihilate our Dramatic Society in the lyceum next week. They are going to debate a question about dramatic exhibitions, I understand."

"Oh, I had heard of that," replied Nat. "We seem to be of much consequence just now. I hardly thought we were able to create such a commotion."

"It seems we are," said Frank, "so you may expect to be finished within a week. Better write your will, and prepare to be made mince-meat of."

"The rest of you will come in for a share," said Nat, "so I shall have a plenty of company, and 'misery loves company' they say."

"But you are the chief sinner," said Frank, smilingly. "You started the thing, and carried off all the glory of performing, so you will have to shoulder the consequences."

"Not a very heavy burden, I am thinking," responded Nat. "I see no need of making such a fuss about a trifle, just as if we boys would spoil the whole town! If Shakspeare were alive he might write another comedy on it like 'MUCH ADO ABOUT NOTHING.' If the town is so dependent on us, I think they ought to make us the fathers of it."

The truth was, that the Dramatic Society had created quite a commotion, as we saw, in part, in a previous chapter. The good people of the village were afraid of the consequences, as well they might be, and the matter was discussed in many family circles, in social gatherings, in the street and other places, until so much interest was awakened on both sides, that the subject was introduced into the town lyceum.

In the hall that was dedicated when Nat was twelve years old, and where he heard the address upon the life and character of Count Rumford by which he was so much impressed, there was a lyceum sustained by the citizens. It was here that the subject of dramatical exhibitions was introduced by a proposition to discuss the following question,

"ARE DRAMATICAL EXHIBITIONS BENEFICIAL TO SOCIETY?"

No question had elicited so much interest as this, pro and con, so that a large attendance was confidently expected.

"Are you going to hear the Dramatic Society used up to-night?" inquired Marcus of Nat, on the day of the proposed discussion.

"Certainly; I am curious to see how the thing will be done. I wouldn't fail of it for any thing. Let us all go, and save the pieces if we can."

"I expect they are preparing for a warm debate, from all I hear; and there will be a crowd there," said Marcus.

Nat and his boon companions were at the hall in good season, to secure seats near the debaters. The hall was filled by the time the hour for opening had arrived, and a spicy time was expected. The president called the meeting to order, the records of the last meeting were read, and other preliminaries disposed of, when the question for discussion was announced. Mr. Bryant, an intelligent and influential man, opened the debate, and remarked, in substance, as follows:

"It is enough to know the origin of theatrical exhibitions. According to the best authorities, when theatrical exhibitions were first given, an old cart was the stage, the chief actor was a coarse mimic or clown, the music was discoursed by itinerant singers, and the poem itself was a motley combination of serious and ludicrous ideas. These performances were first given in honor of the god of wine, Bacchus, which accounts, I suppose, for the fact that a theatre cannot live without a bar. On certain festive days, they acted these plays often in the most indecent manner, with drunkenness and debauchery abounding—scenes which are re-enacted in theatres at the present day. Now, they have a more splendid stage, within a costly, spacious building, but there is little or no improvement in the purity of the play and its incidentals. It is just as demoralizing now as it was then, and has been so in every age of the world. For that reason, such exhibitions have been suppressed, at times, in some countries, and this was the case, at one period, in our own land."

Mr. Bryant was followed by a gentleman on the other side of the subject, but, for a reason that will be obvious to the reader before he gets through the chapter, we shall not report the arguments in the negative.

Another speaker said "that the characters of the actors were loose, exceedingly so; and if the audience could learn something of human nature there, it was only the debasing side of it. It is generally true that actors lend their influence to intemperance, licentiousness, and irreligion. They do not patronize Sabbath schools, churches, and other Christian institutions, but they patronize bars, gambling saloons, and houses of ill-fame. Many of those men even who go to the theatre, would be quite unwilling to introduce actors to the society of their sons and daughters. They are so well convinced that this class are corrupt and unprincipled, that they would exclude them from the fireside."

Another speaker, in the affirmative, said: "As a general thing, dramatic literature is immoral and debasing. I admit that the tragedies of Shakspeare are a pattern of classic elegance and dignity, yet there are passages even in his works that never should be read or spoken in the hearing of others. In them vice is often stripped of its deformity, while virtue is made to appear to disadvantage. The youth who witnesses a play where vice is made to appear as an indiscretion rather than a sin, is likely to think less of virtue, and more favorably of vice. An English scholar has taken pains to read all the plays of the stage of England, and mark all the profane or indecent passages unfit to be read or spoken in a public assembly, and he has found *seven thousand*. During the reign of King James the First, an act was passed 'For the preventing and avoiding the great abuse of the holy name of God in stage-plays.' Addison condemned the theatre 'for ridiculing religion, and for representing the rake and debauchee as the true gentleman.' It is vain to attempt to defend the moral character of dramatic writings."

The first speaker rising to address the audience the second time, said, "that the class of persons who generally patronize the theatre are the most frivolous and useless part of the community. Moral and religious citizens do not lend it their influence, but those who are indifferent or hostile to Christian institutions. Fathers and mothers who are careless of the example they set their children; vain followers of the fashions, who think more of a golden trinket than they do of virtue; idle and dissipated hangers-on of society; fast young men in the road to ruin; vicious young women; dissolute men, whose vices would horrify every sensitive heart were they uncovered; with a sprinkling, perhaps, of better people who forget, for the time being, what company they are in;—these constitute the principal patrons of the stage. Now, then, this single fact is enough to brand the character of theatres as corrupt and pernicious. There is not a person in this hall who would think well of the principles of a man of whom you might be told, 'he is an habitual theatre-goer.' You would infer that his principles were loose, and, in nine cases out of ten, your inference would be correct."

Thus the usual arguments against theatres were quite thoroughly pressed, and were met by the usual ones on the opposite side, though it was evident that the negative realized they had a difficult subject to defend.

Nat listened to the discussion with constantly increasing interest and excitement. His face became flushed, and a nervous tremor passed over his body. At length his frame fairly shook with the excitement under which he was laboring, and Frank, who was sitting by his side, observed it.

"What is the matter with you, Nat?" whispered Frank. Nat made no reply, but continued to catch every word that was uttered. He was evidently dissatisfied with the defence of the theatre by the negative side, and thought that a better plea for it might be made.

"I say, Nat, what's the matter?" whispered Frank again; "got the fever and ague?"

Nat kept his eyes fixed, and did not even bestow a nod of the head upon Frank's inquiry, and the moment the question was given to the audience for general debate,—according to the custom,—Nat started to his feet.

"Mr. President," said he, and every head was up, and every eye fixed, at the sound of his voice. All were astonished that he should presume to speak on that floor; they would scarcely have been more surprised if a strange debater had dropped down through the plastering into the audience. But Nat went on to say, in substance,

"I have listened to the discussion of the question before us with mingled feelings of interest and surprise. Much that has been said I can most cordially respond to, while some of the arguments upon the affirmative do not appear to me legitimate or just. Every subject should be treated fairly, and especially one like this, which is so apt to encounter superstition and prejudice. It is no objection, in my mind, to an enterprise, that it had a lowly origin, any more than it is for an honest and noble man to have descended from ignoble parents. If a man will work his way up from poverty and obscurity by his indomitable energy and perseverance, until he carves his name with scholars and statesmen on the temple of fame, it is the climax of meanness in any one to twit him of his humble origin, and hold him up to ridicule because his parents are poor and unhonored. And so when the gentleman tells us that the theatre was born in a cart, and was originated by those who had neither learning nor character, it is no argument against it, in my view, when I see the rank to which it has attained. The cart has given place to the marble edifice, decorated in the highest style of art, and the place of the untutored street- singer and clown is filled by the queen of song and the prince of orators. The play is no longer devoid of literary character, but is invested with a classic elegance which only the gifted intellect of Shakspeare could impart. What is it that has elevated dramatic entertainments from the cart to the costly temple? Human meanness could not do it, nor human policy alone. It has been accomplished by the intrinsic value to be found in such dramas as those composed by Shakspeare, and that justly entitles them to something nobler than a contemptuous sneer.

"I do not presume to defend theatres as they are, with all the vices that attach to the present manner of conducting them. I admit that the actors are no better than they should be, and that intemperance and licentiousness may be countenanced by them. But when it is intimated that all this is necessarily and inevitably so, I repel the insinuation. Do not gentlemen know that the names of certain actors are associated with all that is pure in character and noble in purpose? Were Garrick and Siddons men of corrupt lives, unworthy to hold an honorable place in society? Who can point to the first line or word ever penned to stigmatize these men? So long as we can refer to them as pure and upright actors, it will be true that corruption does not necessarily belong to the stage.

"I would have intoxicating drinks forever excluded from the theatre, and every possible measure adopted to prevent moral corruption of every kind. I would take the play out of the hands of the base and profligate, and give it to those who are virtuous and true. I would expunge every profane and vulgar word and thought from both tragedy and comedy, leaving nothing that is unfit to be said in the ear of the purest men and women, and then I see not why the stage might not become a medium of innocent pleasure, and intellectual culture. It is bad now, because it is in the hands of bad men. When the virtuous control it, we may expect that its character will be changed.

"When it is said, as it has been on this floor to-night, that nothing good can be learned at a theatre, even as it is at the present time, I must beg to dissent from the opinion. I can testify from actual experience, that much can be learned there of human nature, and much that belongs to the art of speaking. I do not say that many people go to the theatre to learn these things, but I do say they might learn them if they would. Even admitting that the baser side of human nature alone is seen on the stage, a man may learn something from that if he will. As in the low groggery, a pure man may behold to what awful degradation the use of strong drink may reduce its victims, and derive therefrom an argument for temperance that is irresistible, so the exhibitions of the stage may show a pure-minded man how revolting he may become by yielding to the power of his lowest appetites and passions. If he visits such a drinking place to minister to a depraved appetite, and carouse with others, he will go to ruin himself; but if he goes there to acquire the knowledge to which I have referred, he will make a valuable accession to his information and principles. In like manner, if a person goes to the theatre simply to be amused, or for a more dishonorable purpose, he may be corrupted by what he sees and hears; but if he goes for the higher object I have named, he will probably escape contamination."

In this strain Nat proceeded for twenty minutes or more, filling the audience with surprise and wonder. He waxed warmer and warmer, as he advanced, and spoke in a flow of eloquence and choice selection of words, that was unusual for one of his age. No one in the hall had ever listened to such a display of oratorical ability on the part of a youth like him. The most strenuous opposers of the theatre almost overlooked the weakness of Nat's argument in their admiration of his eloquence. It was so unexpected that the surprise alone was almost sufficient to bewilder, them. His mother was in the audience, and her heart leaped into her mouth, as she was first startled by the sound of his voice. She was almost indignant that her boy should attempt to speak in that hall, before such an audience. She expected every moment that he would break down, to his own disgrace and others. But he spoke on, never hesitating for choice words, and put an earnestness and power into every sentence that amazed her. She could scarcely believe what she saw and heard. She was well satisfied with her son when he concluded his speech.

"Nat will make a second Daniel Webster," said the agent of the factory to a friend, as he was going out of the hall.

"I am surprised at his eloquence," replied the friend addressed. "I never heard the like in my life by one of his age."

"We must get him to join the lyceum at once, and bring him out before the public," said the agent.

"That would be an excellent idea, I think; and there will be a great desire to hear him again. I am sure I would like to hear him discuss another question."

"Nat has always been a close student," continued the agent. "When he has not been learning from books, he has studied men and things; and I have expected he would make his mark."

This speech set everybody in the village to talking. Nothing had occurred for a long time that caused so much remark and excitement. The surprise and interest it created remind us of Patrick Henry's first plea, of which Nat himself spoke to Charlie, as we saw in a former chapter. The description which Mr. Wirt gives of it is so applicable to the case before us, that we shall quote it.

"His attitude, by degrees, became erect and lofty. The spirit of his genius awakened all his features. His countenance shone with a nobleness and grandeur which it had never before exhibited. There was a lightning in his eye that seemed to rive the spectator. His action became graceful, bold and commanding; and in the tones of his voice, but more especially in his emphasis, there was a peculiar charm, a magic, of which any one who ever heard him will speak as soon as he is named....

"In less than twenty minutes they might be seen in every part of the house, on every bench, in every window, stooping forward from their stands, in death-like silence, their features fixed in amazement; all their senses listening and riveted upon the speaker, as if to catch the last strain of some heavenly visitant....

"The jury seem to have been so completely bewildered, that they lost sight, not only of the act of seventeen hundred and forty-eight, but that of seventeen hundred and fifty-eight also; for thoughtless even of the admitted right of the plaintiff, they had scarcely left the bar, when they returned with a verdict of *one penny damages*. A motion was made for a new trial; but the court, too, had now lost the equipoise of their judgment, and overruled the motion by a unanimous vote. The verdict and judgment overruling the motion, were followed by redoubled acclamations, from within and without the house.

"The people, who had with difficulty kept their hands off their champion, from the moment of closing his harangue, no sooner saw the fate of the cause finally sealed, than they seized him at the bar, and in spite of his own exertions, and the continual cry of order from the sheriff and the court, they bore him out of the court house, and raising him on their shoulders, carried him about the yard in triumph."

Nat was not carried out of the hall like Patrick, but if his companions and some others, could have acted their own pleasure, a similar scene would have taken place. The reader can scarcely fail to trace some connection between his early familiarity with the life of Patrick Henry, and this brilliant chapter of his experience before the large audience in the town hall. It looks very much as if the reading of that book made a permanent impression upon his mind. It shows, also, that he had not studied the manners of public speakers in vain.

"You couldn't do that again if you should try," said Charlie to Nat, at the close of the meeting. "You was inspired to-night."

"Inspired with respect for our dramatic society," answered Nat, with a laugh. "I thought I would not let it die without one struggle."

"Well," said Frank, "we can afford to let it give up the ghost now, after such a glorious funeral oration over it. But I thought you was having the shaking palsy before you got up to speak."

"It was only the debaters shaking a little interest into me," replied Nat. "They made the spirit move, that's all."

The reader must not infer that opposers of the theatre changed their views in consequence of Nat's argument. For no argument can be framed that will defend the stage from the charge of being a great public evil. In another place we have said enough to show that the ground of his defence was fallacious, though he uttered sentiments which he then sincerely believed. It is certainly no strong defence of the drama that it has risen from the cart to the marble palace, for sin, in some of its grossest forms, thus ascends from a revolting to a gilded degradation. Nor does it avail much to point to here and there a virtuous Garrick among stage-players, when we know that there are a hundred worthless, corrupt actors to one Garrick. And in respect to the possibility of making the theatre respectable, we have seen that it has been repeatedly tried, and failed.

But the audience fell in love with Nat's eloquence. They were charmed by its gracefulness and power. It was that which won their hearts. The result was, that nearly every one became satisfied with his good intention in going to the theatre, and originating dramatic entertainments in the village. It was apparent that it was done for his own personal improvement. He was invited to connect himself with the citizens' lyceum, where he surprised and pleased his friends many times thereafter, by the ability and eloquence with which he discussed different subjects.

The Dramatic Society was relinquished, and the general interest manifested in it was transferred to the town lyceum. A wider and more important field of effort was now open to test Nat's endowments and acquisitions; and he rapidly advanced by making the most of every opportunity.

CHAPTER XXIV.

ANOTHER STEP.

"What are you doing here, Nat?" inquired Charlie, one day, as he entered the carpenter's shop where he was at work with his father.

"I am going to run a partition through here to make a new study for me. Father has given me liberty to use this part of the shop."

"It will make a cozy room," said Charlie, "though it is a little lower down in the world than your other study. It seems you are really going to be a student and nothing else. You must look out that Mother Lane's prophecies are not fulfilled," the last sentence being intended for a sly appeal to Nat's good nature.

"I expect to do a good deal of work yet," replied Nat; "at least, I shall be obliged to work until I find the way to wealth as plain as the way to market. I shall study part of the time, and work the remainder."

At this time Nat had resolved to devote a larger portion of his time to study, and labor only enough to pay his own way along, and provide himself with books—a plan in which his parents cheerfully acquiesced. He went on and finished off his study in his father's shop, and furnished it as well as his limited means would allow. A table, two or three chairs, his scanty library, and a couch on which he slept nights, constituted the furniture of this new apartment. It was more convenient for him to lodge in his study, since he could sit up as late as he pleased, and rise as early, without disturbing any one.

Now he ceased to labor constantly in the machine shop, and worked at his trade only a few months at a time, enough to support himself while pursuing his studies. Occasionally he labored with his father, and played the part of a carpenter.

Charlie was anxious to see the new study when it was completed, and he availed himself of the earliest opportunity to look in upon Nat.

"Here you are, in a brown study. This is capital—I had no idea you would have so good a room as this, Nat. Did you do all this yourself?"

"Certainly; have you any criticisms to offer? You look as if you hardly credited my word."

"I guess your father was round about home," said Charlie, pleasantly.

"But he did not drive a nail, nor plane a board."

"A carpenter, then, with all the rest," added Charlie. "I suppose now the library will be read up pretty fast."

"Not so fast as you imagine. I could never begin with you in reading books. You have read two to my one, I should think."

"Not so bad as that; and it is a poor compliment if it were true, for too much reading is as bad as too little, I expect. The difference between you and me is very plain; *you* read and study to have something to use; and *I* read for the pleasure of it."

"It is true," answered Nat, "that I try to make use of what I learn, though I enjoy the mere pleasure of study as well as you do. But when a person learns something, and then makes use of it, he will never forget it. I might study surveying a whole year in school, but if I did not go out into the fields to apply what I learned to actual practice, it would do me little good; and it is so with every thing."

"There is a good deal of truth in that," replied Charlie; "but there is a difference in the ability of persons to use what they acquire. Some persons have a very poor way of showing what they know."

It was true that Nat did not gorge his mind by excessive reading. Some readers can scarcely wait to finish one book, because they hanker so for another. They read for the mere pleasure of reading, without the least idea of laying up a store of information for future use. Their minds are crammed all the time with a quantity of undigested knowledge. They read as some people bolt down a meal of victuals, and the consequences are similar. The mind is not nourished and strengthened thereby, but is rather impaired finally by mental indigestion.

Coleridge divides readers into four classes. "The first," he says, "may be compared to an hour-glass, their reading being as the sand; it runs in, and it runs out, and leaves not a vestige behind. A second class resembles a sponge, which imbibes every thing, and returns it nearly in the same state, only a little dirtier. A third class is like a jelly-bag, which allows all that is pure to pass away, and retains only the refuse and the dregs. The fourth class may be compared to the slave in the diamond mines of Golconda, who, casting aside all that is worthless, preserves only the pure gem." Nat was a reader of the latter class, and, at the same time, saved every gem for *use*. He had no disposition to *hoard* knowledge, as the miser does his gold. He thought it was designed for use as really as a coat or hat—an idea that does not seem to have entered the heads of many youth, of whom it may be said, "their apparel is the best part of them."

It is as necessary to have a fixed, noble purpose behind a disposition to *read*, as behind physical strength in secular pursuits, otherwise what is read will be of comparatively little service. The purpose with which a thing is done determines the degree of success therein, and the principle applies equally to reading. Nat's purpose converted every particle of knowledge acquired into a means of influence and usefulness, so that he made a given amount of knowledge go further towards making a mark on society than Charlie. The latter usually mastered what he read, and he made good use of it, as the end will show, only it was done in another channel, and in a more private way. He could not have made so deep and lasting an impression on those around him as Nat, with even more knowledge, if he had tried.

"What work are you reading now, Nat?"

"Burke's Essay on the Sublime and Beautiful," replied Nat, taking up the volume from the table. "It is a splendid work."

"I never read it," added Charlie; "the title is so magnificent that I never thought I should like it. *My* head is not long enough for such a work."

"You don't know what it is. It is one of the most practical and useful volumes there is. It is not so taking a book for rapid reading as many others; but it is a work to be *studied*."

"What is the particular use of it?"

"Its use to me is, the information it gives concerning those objects and illustrations that have the most power over the hearts of men in speaking and writing. I should think it must aid a person very much in the ability to illustrate and enforce a subject."

"I suppose you are right," said Charlie, "but it is all gammon to me. That is what helped you to illustrate and enforce the claims of our Dramatic Society in the lyceum, was it?" meaning no more than a joke by this suggestion.

"No; I never read it much until recently," answered Nat.

"Well, I thought you had some of the *sublime* in that speech, if you had none of the *beautiful*," continued Charlie in a vein of humor. "I concluded that Burke might have helped you some, as I thought it hardly probable that Nat did it alone."

"What do you think you should do, Charlie, if you had not me to make fun of?" asked Nat. "You would have the dyspepsia right away. It is altogether probable that I was made to promote your digestion."

"Very likely," replied Charlie, assuming a grave appearance. "I believe they administer rather powerful medicine for that disease. But they say you go to college now," and here his seeming gravity was displaced by a smile. "When are you going to graduate?"

"About the time you know enough to enter," answered Nat, paying back in the same coin.

Charlie was much amused at this turn, for his allusion to college was in a jesting way, occasioned by the fact that Nat had obtained permission to use the library of Cambridge College, to which place he frequently walked to consult volumes. It was a great advantage to him, to enjoy the opportunity to examine works which he could not possess on account of his poverty, and such works, too, as the library of his native village did not contain. It was quite a walk to Harvard College, but necessity made it comparatively short and pleasant to Nat. Many times he performed the trip to settle some point of inquiry, or compass some difficult subject; and the journeys proved to him what similar walks did to Count Rumford many years before. He, also, was accustomed to visit the Athenæum in Boston, at this period of his life, where he spent some pleasant and profitable hours. To many youth it would seem too great an outlay of labor to make for an education; but to Nat it was a cheap way of obtaining knowledge. He was willing to make any sacrifice, and to perform almost any labor, if he could add thereby to his mental stature. Often a volume would completely absorb his thoughts upon a given subject, and he could not let it alone until he had thoroughly canvassed it; and this was one of the elements of his success—a power of application, in which all the thoughts were concentrated on the subject before him. It was thus with Hugh Miller from his boyhood. As an instance, his biographer relates, that, on one occasion he read a work on military tactics—a subject that one would think could scarcely command his attention—and he was so thoroughly controlled by the desire to understand the military movements described, that he repaired to the sea-shore, where he got up an imposing battle between the English and French, with a peck or half bushel of shells, one color representing one nation, and another color the other nation. Time after time he fought an imaginary battle with shells, until he definitely understood the military tactics described in the volume which he read.

Sometimes the perusal of a volume starts off the reader upon a career that is really different from that which the book describes. By its hints or suggestions, it awakens the powers to some incidental subject, upon which they seize with an earnestness and devotion that cannot fail of success. Thus, when William Carey read the "Voyages of Captain Cook," he first conceived the idea of going upon a mission to the heathen world. There was information imparted in that volume, which, in connection with the marvellous adventures and success of the great voyager, fired his soul with the determination to carry the gospel to the perishing.

Nat had such a mind, and difficulties rising mountain high could not hinder him from examining a subject that absorbed his thoughts. A walk of ten miles to see a book, the sacrifice of an evening's entertainment at a party of pleasure, or the loss of a night's sleep, never stood between him and the information he earnestly desired. His unwavering purpose surmounted all such obstacles in the attainment of his object.

CHAPTER XXV.

EULOGY BY JOHN QUINCY ADAMS.

One of the brief periods in which Nat worked at his trade, after he commenced to study more systematically, was spent on the Mill Dam in Boston. At a machine-shop there, he pursued his business a short time, for the purpose of earning the means to defray his expenses while studying.

"John Quincy Adams is to deliver a eulogy on Madison at the old Federal Street Theatre to-morrow," said one of the hands.

"At what time?" inquired Nat.

"Ten o'clock is the time announced for the procession to form. It will probably be twelve o'clock before they get ready for the eulogy."

"I would go," said Nat, "if I had my best clothes here. I could go without losing much time at that hour."

"Did you ever hear John Quincy Adams?"

"No; and that is one reason why I wish to hear him. I have heard many of the distinguished men, but I have never had the opportunity to hear him. I think I shall go as I am."

"And have a representation of the machine-shop there," said his companion. "The nabobs will think you are crazy to come there without your broadcloth."

"Perhaps they would think my broadcloth was too coarse if I should wear it. But if they go to see my suit instead of hearing the eulogy, they are welcome to the sight."

"You will have to lose more time than you expect to; for there will be such a crowd that you cannot get in unless you go early; and you will have to go without your dinner too."

"Dinner is nothing," replied Nat. "It will not be the first time I have gone without my dinner, and supper too. I can leave here at half past eleven o'clock and be in season for the eulogy, and find a place to hear into the bargain. A very small place will hold me at such a time."

"But I prefer a chance to breathe when I can have it as well as not. It is no pleasure to me to go into such a crowd to hear the best speaker in the world. But every one to his taste."

"Yes," responded Nat; "and my taste is right the reverse. I would suffer a pretty good squeezing, and go dinnerless besides, to hear John Quincy Adams speak. I shall try it anyhow."

Nat was usually quite particular in regard to his personal appearance on public occasions. If his best suit had been at hand, he could not have been persuaded to go to hear the eulogy in his working apparel. But he was at work here only a short time, and was at home on the sabbath, so that he provided himself with only his laboring suit. And now we see how strong was his desire to hear the distinguished statesman; for it overcame his regard for his personal appearance so far that he was willing to appear in that assembly wearing his machine-shop apparel, rather than forego the pleasure of an intellectual pastime.

At the appointed time, on the day of the eulogy, Nat dropped his tools, and proceeded to wash himself, and make ready to go.

"Then you are determined to go?" said his companion.

"Yes; I never shall have a better chance to hear the sage of Quincy. I would like to show him a little more respect by donning my best suit if I could, but as it is, he must take the will for the deed."

"You'll cut a dash there among the gentry, I reckon, and perhaps receive more attention than the orator himself. They'll think you are some fellow who has got into the wrong pew."

"You had better conclude to go with me," said Nat, "and enjoy the sight. You will never know how much of a sensation I do create unless you are there to see."

"I'd rather be excused," replied his companion. "I can imagine enough here; besides I like a good dinner too well to go."

Nat hastened to Federal Street, and found the people crowding in very rapidly, and the exercises about commencing. He joined the throng, and was soon borne along with the current into the spacious building. If he had actually wanted to have skulked into some corner, it would have been impossible; for the assembly was so dense that he had no alternative but to remain stationary, or to be carried along by the mass. It so happened that he joined the multitude just in season to be borne well along into the area of the building, in front of the rostrum; and there he was in his working apparel, in full view of hundreds of eyes. Yet he scarcely thought of his clothing in his eagerness to hear the eulogy. It was upon the character of one with whose political life he was quite familiar, and this circumstance increased his interest. His old suit did not at all impair his sense of hearing, nor obscure the language of the orator. He never heard better in his life, and, in but few instances, never felt himself better paid for his effort to hear an oration.

It was known in the shop, before work began in the afternoon, that Nat had gone just as he was to hear the eulogy, and it created some merriment.

"He is a real book-worm," said one; "he always carries a book in his pocket to read when he is not at work."

"Well, I can hardly make out what he is, for he never says much," said another. "He seems to be thinking about something all the time, and yet he attends to his work. He is a queer genius, I guess."

"He is no ignoramus, you may depend on that," said a third. "A chap with such an eye as his knows his P's and Q's. He says little, and thinks the more."

"And then," added the first speaker, "a fellow who will go without his dinner to hear a speech must have a pretty good appetite for knowledge, unless he is obliged to diet."

"He'll have a good appetite for supper, I'm thinking," said another, rather dryly.

Nat heard the eulogy, and was back again to his work within three hours. There were some smiling faces as he entered the shop, and he could very readily read the thoughts behind them.

"Was you in time?" inquired the fellow-workman with whom he had the conversation about going.

"I could not have hit better," Nat replied, "if I had known the precise minute the eulogy would commence. It was good, too; and a greater crowd I never saw."

"There would not have been room for me if I had gone, then?"

"No; *I* just made out the complement. I took the last place there was, and it was a close fit for me."

"How did you like Mr. Adams?"

"Better than I expected. I had not formed a very exalted idea of his eloquence, perhaps because I have heard Webster and Everett, but he was really eloquent, and spoke evidently without any political or partisan prejudices. He appears older than I expected."

"He is getting to be an old man, and he has been through enough to make him gray long ago."

"I am glad to have heard him," added Nat. "Perhaps I might never have had another opportunity."

This incident is another illustration of the sacrifices Nat would make to hear public speakers, and to acquire knowledge, whenever he could. A commendable enthusiasm is apparent here as elsewhere, in seeking the object desired. All those leading traits of his character, that we have seen were so serviceable to him in other places, appear in this brief experience, while an unquenchable thirst for knowledge lay behind them to goad them on to victory.

CHAPTER XXVI.

THE TEMPERANCE SOCIETY.

In Nat's boyhood the principle of total abstinence was not advocated by the friends of temperance. He was considered temperate who drank intoxicating liquor sparingly, and there were few persons who did not use it at all. But a few years later, at the period of his life to which we have now arrived, the total abstinence theory began to command the public attention. The movement commenced with the New York State Temperance Society, and spread rapidly over the country. It reached Nat's native village, and considerable interest was awakened.

"I have been thinking," said Nat to his companions, when they were together one evening, "that we better form a young people's total abstinence society. That is evidently the only right principle of conducting the temperance reform."

"*I* am ready for it," replied Charlie. "Something ought to be done to stop the evils of intemperance. I understand the adults are going to organize a society, and there will be more interest awakened if we young people have one among ourselves."

"I suppose we can belong to the town society if we choose," said Frank, "though I think there would be more interest, as you say, if we have one among ourselves. I am ready to do either."

"What do *you* say, Marcus?" inquired Nat.

"I say 'amen' to it, with real Methodist unction," answered Marcus, with his usual good humor. "Any way that will smash the decanters and get rid of the rum."

"*You* like it as well as anybody," said James Cole, somewhat pettishly, as he was touched by this last remark of Marcus. "I wouldn't trust you out of sight with a decanter, whether you join the society or not."

"What! are you opposed to it, James?" asked Nat.

"Yes, I am; it is all nonsense to talk about never tasting of liquor again. The whole of you would drink wine at the first party where it is passed around. Not one of you would dare refuse."

"You will have a chance to see," said Frank. "The time is not far off when no one will provide wine for a party, if the total abstinence cause advances, as I believe it will."

"Well, I shall not sign away my liberty," continued James, "by putting my name to a pledge. I shall drink when I please, and stop when I please."

"I have no more intention of signing away my liberty," said Nat, "than you have. But I am not anxious for the liberty of getting drunk and lying in the gutter. I prefer to be free, and know what I am about; for then I can walk the streets without reeling when I please."

"A man has no need to make a beast of himself if he does not join a total abstinence society," said James. "I don't believe in drunkenness any more than you do, and there is no need of drinking to excess."

"That is what every toper said once," answered Nat. "Not one of them expected to become a drunkard, and probably they all thought there was no need of it. When a person begins to drink, it is not certain that he will have the ability to stop."

"Fudge," exclaimed James. "You would make out that a man has no self-respect, and no will to govern his appetite."

"That is exactly what I mean to make out," added Nat. "The habit of using intoxicating drinks nurtures an irresistible appetite, so that there is not one hard drinker in ten who could now stop drinking if he should try."

"Are you green enough to believe that?" asked James, in a tone of derision.

"He is just *ripe* enough to believe it," interrupted Marcus. "A green-horn has a good deal to learn before he can believe the truth;" and this sly hit James felt.

"I suppose that you all expect that *I* shall be picked out of the gutter one day, because I can't control my appetite," said James. "I should think so by your talk."

"For one, I should not be at all surprised," replied Nat, "unless you change your views. You certainly maintain the gutter theory."

"Gutter or no gutter," added James, "I shall not sacrifice my liberty by joining a total abstinence society. I will have people know that there is one child who can drink when he pleases, or let it alone."

It was usual at that time, for youth to drink, as well as adults, on certain occasions. If a company of them were out upon an excursion, or attending a party, they did not hesitate to take a glass of wine, and even something stronger. It was according to the custom of the times. It was fashionable to treat callers to something of the kind, and to furnish it as a necessary part of the entertainment at social gatherings. Nat and his companions were accustomed to accept the glass on such occasions. But they were discriminating enough to perceive that there was danger. They did not dare to trust themselves to sustain the drinking usages of the the day. They had heard public lectures upon the subject, in which the perils of the times, both to the young and old, in this respect, were delineated, and they were wise enough to acknowledge the truth of what they heard. Nat espoused the cause from the beginning, with his usual enthusiasm and invincible purpose.

It was decided to organize a Total Abstinence Society, and arrangements were made to effect the object on the following week. Notice was given accordingly, and many of the young people were spoken with upon the subject. The friends of temperance generally encouraged the movement, as a very hopeful one for the young. Nat, assisted by his companions, drafted a constitution before the evening of organization arrived, in order to facilitate the business. The proposition met with many hearty responses.

On the evening appointed to form the society, as many were present as could be expected, and most of them came resolved to join the society. A few were drawn thither by curiosity, having little sympathy with the movement. The meeting was called to order by one of the number, and a temporary chairman elected.

"Mr. Chairman," said Nat, rising from his seat, "we have met here to-night to organize a Total Abstinence Society, and most of us have come with the intention of joining. In order, therefore, to effect a speedy organization, I will present to the meeting the following constitution, which some of us have prepared, for their adoption or rejection. If the constitution is adopted, it will then be proper to circulate it for signatures, and afterwards proceed to the choice of officers."

Nat read the constitution and by-laws, and they were unanimously adopted, and then circulated for signatures. The pledge was incorporated into the constitution, so that signing that was also signing the pledge.

"I move you now," said Charlie, "that we proceed to the choice of officers." The motion was carried.

"How shall the officers be chosen?" inquired the chairman.

"I move they be chosen by ballot," said Frank. This motion was also carried.

"Please prepare and bring in your votes for president," announced the chairman.

Two or three boys' caps made convenient ballot-boxes, so that this order was soon obeyed.

"Votes all in?" inquired the chairman. "If so, I declare the ballot closed."

After counting the ballots, the president announced the result.

"You have made choice of Frank Martin for your president," said he.

Frank took the chair, and the temporary chairman retired.

"Please prepare and bring in your votes for secretary," said Frank.

The order was speedily executed, and the president declared the ballot.

"You have made choice of Charles Stone for your secretary," and Charles took his place at the table.

The remaining officers were duly elected, and other business performed, and thus the first Total Abstinence Society, in Nat's native place, was started by himself and associates. When we consider how long ago it was, and the perils that surrounded the young at that time, on account of the drinking usages, we must concede that it was a very important event to all who put their names to that constitution and pledge. It probably exerted a moulding influence upon their characters through life. Possibly it saved some of them from a drunkard's grave.

The formation of such a society was calculated to create considerable of a sensation in the village, and to provoke many remarks for and against. The principle of total abstinence was so novel to many, that they thought its advocates must be almost insane. Even some temperance men and women, who had defended the cause on the old ground, concluded that there was more zeal than knowledge in taking such a step. In the grog-shops the subject was discussed with much *spirit*.

"You'll have to shut up shop 'fore long," said one customer to Miles, a rumseller, "if the temperance folks can have their own way."

"I guess they won't have their way," replied Miles. "Very few people will sell their liberty out so cheap. I don't apprehend that it will make much difference with my business, whether they have a temperance society or not."

"You haven't heard how swimmingly the young folks went on the other night, I reckon."

"Yes I have; and that was one of Nat's movements. He's dead set against drinking, they say, but he is welcome to all he can make out of this."

"He better be minding his own business, and not meddle with other people's affairs. They say he studies more than he works now; but if he had been compelled to work on at his trade, it would turn out better for him and all concerned."

"Nat is a smart feller," said the rumseller; "but he'll have to be a good deal smarter before he can get many people to say they'll never drink."

"That's certain," responded the customer. "There is no use in trying to do what can't be done. But boys are getting to know more than their fathers in these ere times. I 'spose there are some folks who would like to tell us what we shall eat and wear, and what we shan't."

"I wonder if Jim Cole joined the society?" inquired the rumseller.

"Jim! no! you wouldn't ketch him to make such a dunce of himself. He believes in using a little when he wants it, and that's my doctrine."

"Jim is steady as a deacon natrally," continued the vender, "and I didn't know but he might be influenced by Nat to join."

"He didn't; for he told *me* that he shouldn't sign away his liberty for anybody, and he said that he told Nat, and the other fellers, that they would drink wine at the first party they went to."

"He was wrong there, I'm thinking," answered the rumseller; "for Nat is independent, and he don't back out of any thing he undertakes. He'll be the last one to give it up."

"Doesn't Jim patronize you sometimes?"

"Yes; he occasionally drops in, and takes a little; but Jim doesn't favor hard drinking. He thinks that many men drink too much."

If all the remarks and discussions that were consequent upon the organization of the Total Abstinence Society, could be collected, the result would be a volume. But we must be satisfied with this single illustration, and pass on.

The members of the society studied to know how to make it interesting and prosperous. Various plans were suggested, and many opinions were advanced.

"Let us invite Nat to deliver a lecture," said Frank to Charlie. "He will prepare a good one, and it will interest the people in our movement."

"I had not thought of that," answered Charlie. "Perhaps it would be a good plan. But do you suppose he would do it?"

"I think we could urge him to it," replied Frank. "He likes to speak as well as he does to eat, and a little better; and I know that he can give a capital lecture if he will."

"I think it might be the means of inducing more of the young people to join the society," continued Charlie. "The more popular we make it, the more readily some of them will join us."

"I will go and see Nat at once about it if *you* will," said Frank. "If he does it, the sooner he knows about it the better."

They went to see Nat, and found him in his study. The subject was duly opened, and, after some urging, he consented to deliver a public lecture. At the meeting of the Society on that week, a formal invitation was voted to Nat, and the time of the lecture appointed.

At that time, it required much more decision, perseverance, and moral principle, to espouse the temperance cause than it does to-day. It was a new thing, and many looked with suspicion upon it. Of course, it was a better test of Nat's principles and purpose, than such a movement would be now. That it was a good stand for him to take, and one suited to tell upon his future character, we need scarcely say. It is an important event when a youth of this day resolves that he will never tamper with intoxicating drinks—and that he will pledge his word and honor to this end. It was a far more important event *then*. And when we look upon that group of youth, conferring together upon the claims of the total abstinence principle, and their resolve to adopt it in the face of opposition, we can but record it as one of the most hopeful and sublime events of Nat's early life.

CHAPTER XXVII.

THE TEMPERANCE LECTURE.

The news that Nat would give a lecture on the subject of temperance soon spread through the town, and both the friends and the foes of the cause discussed the anticipated event.

"So it seems that Nat is going to preach temperance to us," said a customer of Miles, the rumseller. "I should think the little upstart thought he was going to reform the town."

"Nat is no upstart I assure you; but he is going a little too fast now," replied Miles. "He is young, however, and he will learn some things in a few years that he don't know now."

"I 'spose every dog must have his day," continued the customer, "and so it must be with timp'rance. It will have its run, and then die a nat'ral death. But it makes me mad to see folks meddle with what is none of their business. Just as if a man hadn't a right to drink when he is a mind to!"

"It's a free country yet," answered Miles, "and all these reformers will find it out before long. But shall you go to hear Nat lecture?"

"I go!" exclaimed the customer. "You won't ketch this child there, I can tell you. Do you 'spose I would go to hear what I don't believe? It's all nonsense, the whole of it, and it shan't have my support."

"I can't agree with you on that point," replied Miles. "*I* sometimes go to hear what I don't believe, and I guess *you* do. I think I shall go to hear Nat if I can leave. I want to see how he makes out!"

"You may go for all I care," added the customer, "and find yourself insulted and abused as rumsellers usually are in such lectures."

On the evening of the lecture, Miles actually went to hear it, and there was a good number of his customers present. Curiosity to hear Nat overcame their opposition to the cause, for the time being, so that they were drawn thither. A lecture by any one else would not have called them out, but the attraction now was too great to be resisted. The hall was crowded with the old and young, and there was not a vacant place for another.

The subject of Nat's lecture was "The Fifteen Gallon Law," which was then agitating the public mind. It was a new movement by the advocates of temperance, and its friends and foes were arrayed against each other for a hard contest. Nat rejoiced in the movement, and therefore prepared himself to defend the law. We will give, in substance, his argument.

After portraying the evils of intemperance in language and eloquence that riveted the attention of the audience, and confirming his statements by unanswerable statistics, he proceeded to say:—

"That something must be done to stay this tide of evil, or we shall become literally a nation of drunkards. It is vain to enact laws to punish the drunkard, and still allow the vender of strong drink to dole out his poison by the glass. For the poor, who need every farthing they earn to purchase bread for their hungry families, will spend their wages at the dram-shop, and leave their children to starve in poverty and degradation. The 'Fifteen Gallon Law' is admirably adapted to save this class. They are never able to purchase intoxicating drinks in larger quantities than by the quart or gallon, so that this law will cut off their supplies. It is true, another class, who possess the means, will not be deterred from purchases by this law, but it is better to save the poor than to save none at all. This appears to be the best thing that can be done at the present time; perhaps sagacious minds will yet discover a universal remedy for this mammoth evil. At any rate, we are urged by the wants of suffering humanity to advocate this law, which may redeem thousands of the poor from their cups and their misery."

The enemies of the law contended that it was introducing "a new principle of legislation," and that while former laws had only "*regulated*" the sale of strong drink, this Fifteen Gallon Law was "*prohibitory*." To this Nat replied,

"That the legislature has power to restrain all trades which are detrimental to the public welfare, and to regulate or prohibit them according as the public good requires. Legislatures have always acted upon this principle, not only in regard to other trades, but also in respect to the traffic in alcoholic drinks. As long ago as 1680, when the public attention was first directed to the evils of intemperance, a law was enacted *prohibiting* the sale of a less quantity than 'a quarter cask,' by unlicensed persons. It also *prohibited* all sales after nine o'clock in the evening, and sales at any time to known drunkards. By this law landlords were obliged to suppress excessive drinking on their premises, and not to allow persons to sit in their bar-rooms drinking and tippling. In 1682, intemperance prevailed to such a degree among sailors, that a law was passed forbidding the sale of liquors to this class, except on a written permit from the master or ship-owner. In 1698, a statute was framed prohibiting all sales to 'any apprentice, servant or negro,' without a special order from the master. In 1721 another law was enacted prohibiting sales *on credit* beyond the amount of ten shillings; and the reason assigned for it was, 'for that many persons are so extravagant in their expenses, at taverns and other houses of common

entertainment, that it greatly hurts their families, and makes them less able to pay and discharge their honest, just debts.' In 1787 this rule was rëenacted, and subsequently *all* sales *on credit* were *prohibited*. Seven years after the adoption of the constitution, a statute was passed limiting the sale to twenty- eight gallons by unlicensed persons. The statute of 1818 prohibited the sale of liquors 'to common drunkards, tipplers, and gamesters; and to persons who so misspend, waste or lessen their estates, as to expose themselves or their families to want, or the town to the burden of their support, by the use of strong drink—or whose health is thus, in the opinion of the selectmen, endangered or injured.' Here is prohibition with a vengeance, going much beyond the provisions of the Fifteen Gallon Law, and forbidding the sale to certain persons, and at certain times. A man was even prohibited from asking for credit at the bar, and the landlord could not grant it if he did, without violating a statute of the Commonwealth. How, then, can the enemies of this measure be bare-faced enough to assert that it is disregarding their inalienable rights? How can they assert, with a shadow of truth on their side, that it is introducing 'a new principle of legislation?' There is no other principle involved in this law than that which is found in our statutes controlling the shooting of certain birds, the sale of tainted meat, the location of slaughter- houses, the existence of lotteries, and many other things that might be named
—all showing that the legislature has authority to prohibit whatever the public good requires. That the public good demands the suppression of intemperance, who can deny? It is the greatest scourge of our land, and the world. It sends thirty thousand annually, in our country, to a drunkard's grave. It tenants our almshouses and prisons with its wretched victims, and causes three fourths of all the crimes that fill the calendars of our courts. It swells your taxes more than all other evils combined, and is the nursery of blasted hopes and miseries that language cannot describe. If then, the public good requires the suppression of any vice in our land, it is this."

Thus he disposed of this plea of the rumsellers, to the happy surprise and satisfaction of the friends of temperance. He discussed other topics connected with the law, and which we have not space to consider. For an hour or more he held his audience in breathless interest, by the strain of argument and oratory that he poured forth from his fruitful mind and earnest heart. A more delighted audience never listened before to a temperance lecture. Its depth, power, and compass were more than they expected. A round of hearty applause told plainly how it was received, as Nat uttered the last word, and took his seat.

"There, Nat," said Marcus to him on the following evening, "you did more good last night than all the temperance lecturers who have come to town."

"How so?" inquired Nat, not understanding his meaning.

"They say you fairly convinced Miles, and he is going to stop selling liquor."

"How do you know?" asked Nat, with a very incredulous look. "I shall want pretty good evidence of that before I believe it."

"He has told a half dozen people so to-day, and one of his best customers among the number."

"Who is that?"

"It was Johnson, who pays him as much money in a year as any other man. Johnson got excited, and denounced him and all the friends of temperance in strong language. He called you a 'fool,' and Miles cracked you up in return, and so they had it for a while rather hot, much to the amusement of Mr. Fairbanks, who happened to hear it."

This was gratifying news to Nat, and to all who sympathized with him in the temperance cause; and it needs some further notice. This Johnson was the customer with whom we became acquainted in another place, a bitter opponent of the "Fifteen Gallon Law." Curiosity, as well as appetite, led him into Miles's shop on the morning after the lecture, for he wanted to hear about it. He had learned in some way that Miles went, as he intimated to him, and therefore it was a good place to go for information.

"So you went to hear Nat last night?" he said to Miles, as he entered the shop. "Did he make a temperance man of you?" meaning this inquiry for a jest.

"Nat spoke real well," answered Miles, "and his arguments were so good that I can't answer them. He's a mighty smart chap."

"What did he harp on last night?" inquired Johnson.

"The Fifteen Gallon Law; and he showed how it would remove the evils of intemperance, which he described so correctly and eloquently that I was astonished. I don't see where he has ever learnt so much."

"Larnt it!" exclaimed Johnson; "he larnt it where he did his impudence. I see that he has pulled the wool over your eyes, and you are more than half timperance now."

"All of that," replied Miles, coolly; "I am going to quit rum-selling at once. If I can't get my living in an honest way, then I will go to the poor-house."

"I hope you *will* go there," answered Johnson, starting up from his chair under great excitement. "A man who has no mind of his own ought to go there. I ——"

"I thought you was going to say," interrupted Miles, "that I ought to go there to keep company with the paupers I have made. I am pretty sure I should have you for a companion before long, if you don't alter your hand."

"I never thought you was overstocked with brains," continued Johnson; "but if you will be hoodwinked by that fool of a Nat, you have less than I thought you had. It is great business for a man of your age to give up beat to a boy, and that is all Nat is, though he thinks he's a man."

"Boy or not," answered Miles, "he spoke better last night than any man I ever heard. He is a first-rate orator, and his defence of the 'Fifteen Gallon Law' was unanswerable."

"A feller ought to speak well who has studied as much as he has," said Johnson. "He hain't earnt his salt for two or three years, 'cause he's too lazy to do any thing but look at a book."

"I don't care how much he has studied," answered Miles. "If I had a son who could speak as well as he does, I should be proud of him, though he had done nothing but study for ten years. Your talk is very unreasonable, and you know it; and for that reason, it will not change my opinion of Nat."

"Run arter him, then, to your heart's content," said Johnson, turning to go out, "and be a timperance man if you will,—it'll take more than this to make you decent;" and with these words he left the premises in a rage.

Mr. Miles carried out his determination to cease the traffic in strong drink, and engage in some more honorable business. His unexpected espousal of the total abstinence principle, and the closing of his dram-shop, offended many of the rum fraternity. It was a signal achievement for the temperance cause, however, and for the welfare of the village.

The lecture of Nat won for him an enviable reputation, not only at home, but abroad, and he was soon invited to deliver it in the neighboring towns. Wherever he consented to give it, it was received with decided favor, and the anticipations of hearers were more than realized.

Subsequently he delivered other lectures on the subject of temperance in his native village, and the people soon learned that no lecturer called out so large audiences as he. There was always a desire to hear him; and his sonorous voice, bewitching eloquence, and sensible thoughts, never failed to entertain his auditors.

CHAPTER XXVIII.

SPEECH-MAKING.

At this time Nat occupied a position of honor and influence which few persons of his age ever attain. But let not the reader suppose it was the result of chance, or the consequence of superior talents alone. He was more indebted for it to the studious habits which he formed from twelve to fifteen years of age, than to any thing else. If he had wasted his spare moments then in idleness,—as many boys do,—he never would have surprised the lyceum with a speech of such eloquence, nor been able to entertain an audience on the subject of temperance. The habits of life are usually fixed by the time a lad is fifteen years of age. The habits which Nat had established at this period of life, made him what he was five years later. Those early years of industry and application could not be thrown away without demolishing the fabric that was reared upon them. They were the underpinning of the beautiful structure that so many delighted to view when the busy architect was a little older. For, if it could ever be truthfully said of any one, "he is the artificer of his own fortune," it could be said of Nat. The bobbin boy was father of the young and popular orator.

It is generally true, as we have intimated before, that the influence of habits at ten or fifteen years of age, is distinctly traceable through the whole career of eminent men. Sir James Mackintosh was thirteen years of age when Mr. Fox and Lord North were arrayed against each other on the subject of the American war. He became deeply interested in the matter through their speeches, and from that time concentrated his thoughts upon those topics that contributed to make him the distinguished orator and historian that he became. He always considered that the direction given to his mind, at that early period of his life, settled his destiny. The great naturalist Audubon, was just as fond of birds and other animals, when ten years old, as he was in manhood. He studied natural objects with perfect admiration, and took the portraits of such birds as he particularly fancied. When he was sent to Paris to be educated, away from the beauty and freshness of rural objects, he became tired of his lessons, and exclaimed, "What have I to do with monstrous torsos and the heads of heathen gods, when my business lies among birds?" The foundation of his success as a naturalist was laid in his sparkling boyhood. Benjamin West was made a painter, as he said, by his mother's kiss of approbation, when she saw a picture he sketched, at seven or eight years of age. He became just what he promised to be in his boyhood, when he robbed the old cat of the tip of her tail out of which to manufacture a brush, to prosecute his delicate art. Thus it was with Eli Whitney, who proved himself such a benefactor to mankind by his inventive genius. His sister gives the following account of his boyhood: "Our father had a workshop, and sometimes made wheels of different kinds, and chairs. He had a variety of tools, and a lathe for turning chair-posts. This gave my brother an opportunity of learning the use of tools when very young. He lost no time; but, as soon as he could handle tools, he was always making something in the shop, and seemed not to like working on the farm. On a time, after the death of our mother, when our father had been absent from home two or three days, on his return he inquired of the house-keeper what the boys had been doing? She told him what B. and J. had been about. 'But what has Eli been doing?' said he. She replied that he had been making a fiddle. 'Ah!' added he despondingly, 'I fear Eli will have to take his portion in fiddles.' He was at this time about twelve years old. This fiddle was finished throughout, like a common violin, and made tolerably good music. It was examined by many persons, and all pronounced it to be a remarkable piece of work for such a boy to perform. From this time he was employed to repair violins, and had many nice jobs, which were always executed to the entire satisfaction, and often to the astonishment of his customers. His father's watch being the greatest piece of machinery that had yet presented itself to his observation, he was extremely desirous of examining its interior construction, but was not permitted to do so. One Sunday morning, observing that his father was going to meeting, and would leave at home the wonderful little machine, he immediately feigned illness as an apology for not going to church. As soon as the family were out of sight, he flew to the room where the watch hung, and, taking it down, he was so much delighted with its motions, that he took it all in pieces before he thought of the consequences of his rash deed; for his father was a stern parent, and punishment would have been the reward of his idle curiosity, had the mischief been detected. He, however, put the work all so neatly together, that his father never discovered his audacity until he himself told him many years afterwards."[A] Such was the boyhood of one who invented the *cotton-gin*, made improvements in the manufacture of fire- arms, by which the national government saved, as Mr. Calhoun said "twenty- five thousand dollars per annum," and contributed largely to advance other mechanical arts. How distinctly we can trace, in all these examples, the moulding influence of boyhood upon manhood! And how marked the correspondence between the early life of all these men and that of Nat! Thus it is that the beautiful poem of Longfellow, "The Village Blacksmith," is abundantly illustrated in the biography of both the living and the dead! A few of the verses are:—

"Under a spreading chestnut-tree
    The village smithy stands;
The smith, a mighty man is he,
    With large and sinewy hands;
And the muscles of his brawny arms
    Are strong as iron bands.

"His hair is crisp, and black, and long,
    His face is like the tan;
His brow is wet with honest sweat,
    He earns what e'er he can,
And looks the whole world in the face,
    For he owes not any man.

"Week in, week out, from morn till night,
    You can hear his bellows blow;
You can hear him swing his heavy sledge,
    With measured beat and slow,
Like a sexton ringing the village bell,
    When the evening sun was low.

"Toiling,—rejoicing,—sorrowing,
    Onward through life he goes;
Each morning sees some task begin,
    Each evening sees it close;
Something attempted, something done,
    Has earned a night's repose.

"Thanks, thanks to thee, my worthy friend,
    For the lesson thou hast taught!
Thus at the flaming forge of life
    Our fortunes must be wrought;
Thus on its sounding anvil shaped
    Each burning deed and thought!"

But to return. For some time Nat's attention had been directed to political subjects, and he had been hither and thither to listen to various speakers. At length he became so enthusiastic in support of his own political tenets, that he was urged to undertake political speech-making. There was ample opportunity for the display of his abilities in this way, since the political excitement was strong.

"What do you think," said he to Charlie, "about my engaging in politics? I have been urged to speak at political meetings."

"You better do it," replied Charlie. "You are well qualified for it; and you always have taken an interest in politics ever since you read the Life of Jefferson. Where do they want you should speak?"

"Here, and in other places, too; and I scarcely know what to do about it. In some respects I should like it, and in others I should not."

"Do it, by all means," added Charlie. "It will not interfere much with your studies, as you will speak only in the evening."

"But that will interfere very much with my present plans. It will be on my mind all the time, so that my interest will be divided at least. No one can have too many irons in the fire, and attend to them all. One thing at a time is about as much as any person can do well."

"That may be very true, but why not make that one thing politics? We must have men to manage State affairs, as certainly as to be lawyers, physicians, and ministers. Besides, if I can read you, Nat, you are actually cut out for this sphere of action."

"You don't read me correctly if that is your opinion. There must be a great many unpleasant things in such a life. If the speaking were all, I should like that well enough, but that is a small part of political experience."

"Try it, try it," added Charlie, "and see how you make it go. You need not continue in it longer than you please. I want to see you take the stump once. Perhaps you will make a Democrat of *me*."

Nat met the last remark with a laugh, and said "That is too much to expect. You are a hopeless case,—too incorrigible to be won over to the right side. I relinquished all hope of you a long time ago."

"Now, seriously," said Charlie, "I advise you to speak at political meetings, and I hope you will speak here first. It will be the best thing you can do. If I possessed your abilities for public speaking, I would do it in a minute."

"Perhaps I shall conclude to do so," was Nat's reply, as they separated.

The result was, that Nat decided to address a political gathering in his native town; and soon after he visited some neighboring places on the same errand. He soon acquired a reputation, as the "young orator," and committees waited upon him from towns near and remote. The adventure of one of these committees rehearsed, will show what expectations were awakened by his spreading fame.

A committee, in the town of ——, were instructed to wait upon him, and secure his services at a great political gathering there. Accordingly the committee put on their "Sunday suit," harnessed the horse into the best carriage, and started for Nat's residence. Meeting a man, as they entered the village.

"Where is Esquire —— (meaning Nat)'s office?"

The person addressed did not understand who was meant at first, and asked for the repetition of the inquiry, which was readily granted.

"Oh," answered he, "it is down yonder," at the same time pointing to a street a quarter of a mile distant or more, and scarcely able to control his risibles as he thought of the joke he was about to perpetrate.

"Very much obliged to you," responded the inquirer, at the same time whipping up his horse.

"This is nothing but a carpenter's shop," said one of them, as they reached the place. "We must have misunderstood him."

"It is very evident," said the other, "that we shall have to look further yet. But let us go in and inquire."

So they alighted, and went in.

"We are looking for Esquire ——'s office. A gentleman directed us a short distance back, but we find that we did not understand him."

"Whose office did you say?" inquired Nat's father, who happened to be the person addressed.

"Esquire ——'s office, the young orator we have heard so much about."

Nat's father was very much amused at this turn of matters; but he kept on a sober face, and replied, pointing to Nat, who was planing a board,

"That is the young man you want to see, I suppose."

The committee looked at each other, and then at the black-haired board- planer, with perfect amazement. Their countenances told just what they thought; and if we should write their thoughts out in plain English, they would run thus:

"What! that young fellow the stump orator of which we have been told so much. We better have staid at home, than to risk our party in his hands. Why! he is nothing but a boy. There must be some mistake about the matter."

While astonishment was evaporating from the tops of their heads, and oozing out of the ends of their fingers, Nat had turned away from the bench to welcome the official strangers. There he stood hatless, and coatless, with his shirt-sleeves stripped up to his elbows, and his noble brow wet with perspiration, looking little like one who could sway an audience by the power of his eloquence.

"We are a committee from the town of——instructed to wait on you, and engage you to address a political convention," said one of them, breaking the silence.

"When is the convention?" inquired Nat.

"Two weeks from this time, the 15th day of October."

"I will be there," answered Nat, "and do the best I can for you."

The matter was adjusted, and the committee left, evidently thinking that an orator whose office was a carpenter's shop could not be a remarkable defender of democratic principles. On their way home, they spoke freely to each other of their mistake in engaging one so inexperienced to address the convention. They concluded that it would teach them a good lesson, and that in future they would not risk the reputation of their party in unskilful hands.

It is sufficient to say, that Nat filled the appointment to the satisfaction of the crowd, and the surprise of the committee. Before he had spoken fifteen minutes, the committee discovered that they had misjudged the orator, and that he was, indeed, the youthful champion of their party. His speech fully convinced them that he could address a political assembly a little better than he could plane a board.

[A] A good sketch of Eli Whitney's Life, and the lives of some other self-made men, spoken of in this volume, may be found in "*Biography of Self-Taught Men*," by Professor B. B. Edwards. Every youth in the land ought to read this work, not only for the information it imparts, but for the incentives to "noble, godlike action," which it presents on almost every page.

CHAPTER XXIX.

THE EARLY VICTIM

"I have just heard," said Nat one morning to a neighbor, "that James Cole was frozen to death last night while intoxicated. Is it true?"

"I had not heard of it," replied the neighbor. "Some people at the head of the street were conversing about something that had occurred as I passed, but I did not understand what it was. Perhaps it was that. He has conducted badly for a year past, and I suppose he is a confirmed drunkard, although he is so young."

Just then Frank came along, and, before Nat had time to inquire, proceeded to say, "James Cole came very near freezing to death last night, and the physician thinks it is doubtful whether he will recover."

"How did it happen?" asked Nat.

"He spent last evening at one of the grog-shops, I don't know which, and staid drinking until it was very late; and he was badly intoxicated when he started for home, so that he did not get far before he fell down in the road, and was unable to get up. It was so late that no one came along until this morning, and there he laid senseless all the while, and was completely chilled through when Mr. Bates found him this morning."

"Then Mr. Bates found him?" said Nat.

"Yes; and he could scarcely tell whether he was dead or alive at first. He carried him to his father's immediately, and sent for the doctor as quickly as possible."

"Do you know what time it was when he left the grog-shop?"

"No; but I heard it was very late."

"Well," added Nat, "a man who will sell James Cole liquor until he makes him drunk, and then send him home alone, on such a night as last night was, has no more feeling than a brute. If he should die, that rumseller would be the actual cause of his death."

"Certainly," answered Frank; "it would not have been half so bad to have robbed him of his money, and turned him away without any drink. But I wonder if Jim thinks now of the conversation we had with him about forming the Total Abstinence Society?"

"He has probably found out by this time," replied Nat, "that he can't stop drinking when he pleases, after an appetite for it is acquired. He was very sure that he should never be a drunkard; and that was but little more than two years ago."

"I never expected he would be much, but I had no idea he would come to this so soon," added Frank. "I scarcely ever heard of a person going to ruin so quick."

"James was a very smart fellow, naturally," said Nat. "I once thought he was the most talented fellow of his age in town, and it would have turned out so if he had tried to make anything of himself."

"I think so, too," said Frank. "But he never wanted to be respectable. He always seemed to glory in drinking. He was earning five dollars a day in the machine-shop when they turned him away, and was considered by far the best workman there. He lost his place on account of his intemperate habits; but it never seemed to trouble him. It is my opinion now, that he had a strong appetite for intoxicating drinks at the time we organized the Total Abstinence Society, and for that reason he opposed it."

"His case will be a good defence of the temperance cause," continued Nat, "and I hope the rumsellers will never hear the last of it. I can scarcely see what a person can say in favor of the use and traffic in strong drink, with such an illustration of the evil before them."

The news of James's condition spread through the village, and many received it in a very exaggerated form. Some heard that he was dead, and others that he was near dying, the latter rumor not being far from the truth. Before night, however, it was announced that he was better, and there was hope of his recovery. All sorts of stories were put in circulation about the place of his drinking, and the circumstances attending it. The rumseller very justly came in for his share of condemnation, while he and his allies were disposed to say very little, for the simple reason that there was not much for them to say. Such an instance of degradation in the very dawn of manhood, when the dew of his youth was still upon the victim, was an unanswerable argument for the cause of temperance. He who could close his senses against such an appeal in behalf of sobriety, would take the side of error in spite of the plainest evidence to the contrary. It was not strange, then, that much was said at the fireside, in the streets and shops, and everywhere, concerning the event, nor that the foes of temperance were inclined to be unusually silent.

"Doctor! how is James Cole now?" inquired a gentleman who met him some three or four weeks after the fatal night of drunkenness.

"His case is hopeless," answered the doctor. "He has a hard cough, and to all appearance is in a quick consumption."

"Do you consider it the consequence of his exposure on that night?"

"Certainly, it can be nothing else. If it had been a very cold night he would have been frozen to death in the morning. I did not know that he had become so much of a drunkard until this happened."

"I did," replied the gentleman. "I have seen a good deal of him, and have known something of his habits. I was satisfied, when he was but sixteen or eighteen years of age, that he had an appetite for liquor, and I am not surprised at the result."

"The poor fellow will soon know the worst," added the doctor. "He can't live many weeks at the longest."

"I hope it will prove a warning to the young here," said the gentleman. "The fact is, I wonder sometimes that we do not have more of such cases when the temptations to drink are so common. But *one* ought to be sufficient to move the whole town on the subject."

Not quite twelve weeks have elapsed since the foregoing incident occurred. The bell tolls out its solemn death-knell, and the sable hearse is moving slowly on to the grave-yard. Sad, tearful mourners follow, to lay all that remains of James Cole—the son, and brother—in the silent "narrow house." For the demon-vice has done its worst, and loosed the silver chord, and his youthful spirit has gone before the drunkard's offended God. Alas! what painful memories throng the minds of beholders at the sight of the long, mournful procession on its way to the tomb! Never did a hearse convey more blasted hopes or wasted powers, more abused and withered ties, or dishonored members, to the house of the dead. Within that coffin is the bright promise of youth, the strength of early manhood, parental expectations and love—all blighted by the breath of the destroyer, and laid in as sad a winding-sheet as ever wrapped a tenant of the grave. Oh! how great the woes of intemperance appear, when these appalling realities dash earthly hopes, and send the wretched victim away to that world "from whose bourne no traveller returns!" So thought many as the lifeless form of James Cole was consigned to its kindred dust.

"Another drunkard's grave," said the sexton, as the stones rattled upon the coffin which he proceeded to cover, when the procession had retired; and his remark was addressed to a neighbor who stood by his side.

"Not exactly a drunkard's grave," was the reply. "James was intemperate, but he died of consumption."

"And was not that consumption the consequence of his drunkenness?" inquired the sexton.

"I suppose it was; still I thought we could hardly call this a drunkard's grave, though it is true enough."

"It is too painfully true," added the sexton. "Would that it might be called otherwise; but it cannot be. When you and I are numbered with the dead, this spot will be known by all who have seen James Cole buried to-day, as the drunkard's grave. There are many of them in this yard, but *I* never dug a sadder one than this."

"And I hope you never will another," said the man.

So the sexton buried the sleeper, and turned away to his home. For more than twenty years his dust has been mingling with its native earth, without a stone to mark the spot, nor a flower to tell of hope. But his early companions, whose wiser choice and better resolves allied them to the cause of virtue, know where the early victim was laid, and call it the youthful DRUNKARD'S GRAVE.

CHAPTER XXX

THE END.

Let almost a quarter of a century pass, and inquire, where and what are Nat and his associates now? We have advocated the sentiment throughout these pages, that the character and position of manhood are determined by boyhood and youth. How is it with the group of boys who have figured in the foregoing pages? Does the history of each one verify the truth we have taught? or is even one of the number an exception to the general principle stated?

We have already seen one of this number laid in a drunkard's grave,—the boy who thought he could take the social glass, according to the custom of the times, and still be safe,—the youth who had more confidence in his own strength to resist temptation, than he had in the wholesome counsels of superiors. How speedily the thoughts, habits, and corrupt principles of his youth, wrought his ruin!

Some distance back in the story, we lost sight of Samuel and Benjamin Drake, —the two disobedient, idle, reckless, unmanageable boys, at fifteen years of age. What has been their history? Alas! it is written in letters of shame! The following description of these boys, when they became young men, taken from the records of a State prison, will show that both of them have been there.

"Samuel Drake: 28 years old—blue eyes—sandy hair—light complexion. —— Mass."

"Benjamin Drake: 22 years old—blue eyes—light hair—light complexion— scar on right instep. ——, Me."

We give the true record, except that we use the fictitious names employed in this volume, and withhold the names of the towns from whence they were conveyed to prison.

Five years later to the records of the same prison was added the following:

"Samuel Drake: 33 years old—blue eyes—sandy hair—light complexion— second comer. ——, Mass."

By this it appears that Samuel was twice in the State prison by the time he was thirty-three years of age. What has been his course since that period is not exactly known, though report said, a few years ago, that he ended his life on board a pirate-ship.

But the reader is surprised, perhaps, that Benjamin should become the inmate of a prison; for the last we saw of him was when he was preparing for the ministry—a converted youth, as he thought, of seventeen years. We cannot furnish every link that connects his boyhood and manhood; but the painful story is told, in substance, when it is said that his religion proved like the morning dew, and his early vicious habits returned with redoubled power, so that five years after he attended the prayer-meeting with Frank Martin, he was incarcerated for theft. It is a startling illustration of the force of boyhood's evil habits, often lording it over a man to his shame and ruin, even when he has resolved to lead a better life.

The remainder of this group of boys have proved an honor to their sex, as the principles and habits of their early lives fairly promised.

Frank Martin stands at the head of a public institution, where great responsibilities are devolved upon him, as a servant of the Commonwealth. Strange as it may seem, the institution over which he presides is the one in which his old associates, Samuel and Benjamin Drake, were incarcerated; and Frank himself opened the prison records for the writer to make the foregoing extracts.

Charlie Stone has been connected with manufactures from the beginning, advancing from one post of responsibility to another, employing his leisure time to improve his mental faculties; and he is now the honored agent of one of the wealthiest and most celebrated manufacturing companies of New England, commanding a salary of THREE THOUSAND AND FIVE HUNDRED DOLLARS.

Marcus Treat, perhaps influenced by the example of Nat, devoted his spare moments to self-culture, and made commendable progress before he resolved to quit his trade, and educate himself for the legal profession. Without means of his own, or wealthy friends to aid, he succeeded in his laudable efforts, and, without being able to command a collegiate education, was admitted to the bar. He now occupies a post of honor and influence in a thriving State of our Union, where he is known as one of the most popular members of the bar.

And Nat—what and where is he? He is now known to fame as His Excellency, The Governor of ——, the best State in the Union, which is only one remove from the Presidency of the best country in the world. By his own diligence, industry, perseverance, and self-reliance, he has fully earned the confidence of his constituents. No "lucky stars," no chance-game or accident, can make a Governor out of a bobbin boy; but the noble qualities named can, as if by the power of magic, achieve the wonderful transformation. It is true of him, as the poet has said of all distinguished men,—

"The heights by great men reached and kept
    Were not attained by sudden flight;
But they, while their companions slept,
    Were toiling upward in the night."

And now, ere the youthful reader closes this volume, let him stop and resolve to imitate the bright example of him whom we never more shall dare to call Nat. His business now is so different from that of carrying bobbins, and his position and character so far removed from that of student-boy in his father's attic, that we can only call him HIS EXCELLENCY, as we reverently tip our hat. But the leading characteristics of his youth are worthy of your imitation, whether you desire to pursue the path of knowledge or any other honorable vocation. Are you poor? So was he; poorer than hundreds of the boys who think that poverty stands in the way of their success. Are your advantages to acquire an education small? So were his; smaller than the opportunities of many youth who become disheartened because they are early deprived of school. Are you obliged to labor for a livelihood, so that your "odd moments" are few and far between? So was he; and if ever a lad could be excused from effort on this plea, it was he who toiled fourteen hours per day in a factory, to earn his bread. There is no excuse for non-exertion that will stand before the Bobbin Boy's example—not one. Imitate it, then, by cultivating those traits of character which proved the elements of his success.